... ING SILAS

THE BOYS OF FURY

KELLY COLLINS

BOOK NOOK PRESS

Copyright © 2017 by Kelly Collins

No part of this publication may be reproduced, distributed, or transmitted in any form or by any means, including photocopying, recording, or other electronic or mechanical methods, without the prior written permission of the publisher, except as permitted by U.S. copyright law. For permission requests, contact kelly@authorkellycollins.com.

The story, all names, characters, and incidents portrayed in this production are fictitious. No identification with actual persons (living or deceased), places, buildings, and products is intended or should be inferred. All products or brand names are trademarks of their respective owners.

CHAPTER 1

GRACE

Every day the life I'd known slipped further away from me, and the life I had threatened to swallow me whole.

We entered Fury Consignments, and I rushed to the burled wood coffee table near the entry. "I love this." Its high-gloss shine was perfect for an upscale apartment or a downtown loft. Perfect for my old lifestyle. Maybe if I infused my new life with some reminders of the old one, I wouldn't feel so out of place and lonely.

"It's nice, but ..." Ana flipped over the price tag, and we both gasped.

"Five hundred dollars?" I whisper-yelled. "Who has that kind of money in Fury?" A year ago, I wouldn't have balked at laying down several big bills, but that was when I lived in a modern high-rise, worked as an executive assistant, and made fifty-five grand a year.

"What do you think of this?" I pointed to the ugly-ass table in the corner. It didn't have the beauty, style, or grain of the burled table, but I could get used to it. After all, Fury didn't have the nightlife, the options, or the allure of Denver, but I'd adjusted.

Ana shook her head. "It's fine if your last name is Planter."

I leaned against a ladder-back chair. Tables and lamps, sofas and beds surrounded me, but I knew the consignment store had nothing affordable in my style. The peanut table was the worst. What had happened to me? I used to have good taste, but that was when I'd lived in Denver, dined in fine restaurants, and dated men who wore suits and cologne.

A man in jeans who smelled like hard work came closer. "A pretty fine piece at a good price."

I rubbed my hand around the curve of the table. "All the corners are rounded, which means Blue's head will avoid turning blue when he bumps it." I kissed my five-week-old son's bald melon and breathed in the combination of baby shampoo and innocence. The perfect scent on a perfect boy. Collisions with furniture were in the distant future, but moms took planning seriously. My life was all about him now.

"All these tables are making me think of food. I need to eat." Ana smoothed her hand over her rounded belly.

"Are you kidding me? We just ate," I blurted, before remembering I'd been a one-woman eating machine when I was pregnant. Baby brain was no joke.

"That was an hour ago, and I'm eating for two." She looked around the secondhand shop. It couldn't be helping that there were old signs for Coke and popcorn and something called an Abba Zabba, which seemed to be a sugary delight filled with gooey peanut butter. Even my stomach growled.

"I'll get you real food after we find the perfect table," I said, squatting next to the jumbo wooden peanut and fishing around Blue's baby bag for my stash of protein bars. I was no longer pregnant, but I was always hungry. So was Blue. He never seemed to get enough time at the tit. Even now he stirred in the sling, his mouth suckling toward my breast.

"What about this one?" Ana placed her hand on the round table that sat in the center of the room.

I handed her the snack bar and walked around it. "You think this is better?"

She took a bite of the bar and moaned in appreciation like she hadn't eaten in years. "At least we can do something with this one."

"Like what?" With her designer's eye, Ana could make garbage look grand. "Not that it matters. There's nobody in Fury for me to show it to. Unless you count old man Tucker."

"Bob sure does have a thing for you." Ana skimmed her fingers across the smooth wood.

I nodded and checked out the legs on the table. "He's sweet." Bob hadn't been sweet, he'd been sent straight from heaven, showing up with the crib and diapers out of the blue—part of the reason I named my son Blue.

The second leg of the table wobbled under my grasp, and the whole thing nearly toppled. "Not safe."

Not that I could afford safe. I could hardly afford anything. When I'd moved into the house on Abundant, doors down from Mona and Ana, I had a bed and little else. But within a week, my bungalow was fully furnished. Fury might have had an angry name, but it was a town full of good people.

Ana knelt next to me and wobbled the leg. "Everything's fixable." She brushed her fingers across Blue's light red fuzz. "Do you hear from his dad?"

"The best thing about Trenton Kehoe is his absence." My baby boy didn't look a thing like his dad except for his blue eyes, and I was waiting for them to change. "I do miss men, though." I pulled Blue close to my chest. "What I miss is being held. And, if I'm honest with myself, I miss orgasms." They weren't as good when self-induced. There was no buildup or anticipation. I couldn't fake myself out. I didn't have the willpower to pull myself to the edge and back off just to frustrate me. No, I was quick and efficient when it came to self-pleasure.

"You won't be single forever." She snapped the price tag from the round table and handed it to me. "This is the one."

"You think?" She was right. Given that there were only a handful of coffee tables, this was the one. "I wish picking out a guy was so easy."

A shit-eating grin spread across Ana's face. "So, Bob is definitely out, huh?"

"Did I really move here?" At the time, I'd had nowhere else to go. Now I questioned the sanity of my decision. "I'm a single mother living alone in a dusty mountain town. I have nobody."

We threaded our way through the cast-offs to the register. The sour-faced cashier took the price tag. "I'll need $102.65."

"So much for dining out this month." I handed over my credit card, and Ana pulled me close to her side. She had that thoughtful look about her, the one that usually softened her face before she gifted me with some quote or words of wisdom.

"You're not alone. You have Ryker and me. And don't forget, Ryker is on his way to pick up Silas. They'll be home tomorrow."

"Why tomorrow?" It wasn't that I was desperate to meet the man, although anyone south of sixty was appealing at this point.

"You know, male bonding and all that stuff. Besides, Silas hasn't been back since that day, and Ryker thought he'd ease him into it."

"Seems wise." I couldn't imagine coming back to the place where my parents were slaughtered. "Do you think he'll stay?"

"It's hard to say. I know Ryker wants him to stay. But Silas needs a constant supply of endorphins to keep him happy."

A puff of air rushed from my mouth. "I could show him endorphins." I looked down at my now-sleeping baby. "Nothing ups the blood pressure like a baby with a high-pitched scream at two in the morning."

I wrote down my address and arranged for delivery of the table. It was the only thing that hadn't shown up on my doorstep on its own. Not bad for a woman who'd left everything behind. Somehow my less had turned out to be more in many ways.

The grumble of Ana's tummy was my cue to take her to the diner. It had become our favorite place to eat. That was possibly because it was the only place to eat in Fury.

We walked across the street and slid into our favorite booth in front of the window. It was a good place to watch what life there was in a sleepy town crawl by.

We ordered the special, and I discreetly pulled out my boob for Blue to feast on. Once he was hooked up, I opened three packets of sugar and added them to my tea. I knew I'd pay for this later—anytime I had caffeine or sugar, the baby was up all night—but I needed it. I was exhausted.

"You think our kids will be best friends like us?"

"No doubt." Ana dropped her hand to her stomach. "Maybe mine will be a girl, and they'll fall in love and get married."

"That would be nice," I said in a dreamy way, knowing the reality would be they'd fight like siblings.

My phone rang, breaking my reverie, and once I saw it was my dad, I silenced it and pushed it away. He'd been calling nonstop all day but hadn't left a single message. That meant no emergency. I took another look around the restaurant at all the seemingly functional families.

"Who keeps calling?"

"My dad," I said like I was throwing up the word.

"What's up?" She followed my gaze. Mothers and fathers and kids in tight little units. Grandparents ogling the little ones. "You haven't told them yet?" She reached across the table and snatched my hand into hers. "They're your family. He's their grandson. You have to tell them."

"You're my family." My throat tightened, and my voice cracked. "And you're all I need, which is why I wanted to ask you to be Blue's godmother."

It wasn't how I planned to ask her, but if it got Ana off the subject of my family, then my question served two purposes. I hadn't told my parents a thing. I'd managed to stay one step ahead of them the whole time, but something told me they were hot on my barely affordable Payless pumps.

CHAPTER 2

SILAS

I was the last passenger to exit the plane. I gave a final adjustment to my belt buckle and waved goodbye to the blonde flight attendant. Sarah, I thought, but couldn't remember. I did remember her taste. It still lingered in my mouth.

"I hope you enjoyed your flight." She grinned. "And do come again."

Damn, she was insatiable. Not only had I made it to the mile-high club, she'd taken me to the bathroom three times in the three-hour flight from California. She had a thing for soldiers, and I had a thing for sex. It was a match made in heaven.

Hell, I'd have her pinned on the bathroom sink right now if the cleaning crew didn't have to get inside to empty the tanks.

I flipped my new phone off airplane mode and walked up the aisle.

"You forgot this, sugar." She held out a piece of paper with a phone number on it. "I'll be in town for a few days."

I smiled and tucked the number into my front pocket even though I knew I'd never call. I'd already boarded her craft several times; there was no need for a return trip.

"See you around."

I swung my duffle bag over my shoulder. What I couldn't carry, I didn't need. Life was easier that way. No connections. No ties. Endless motion.

My phone vibrated—a text from Ryker. Besides my first sergeant, he was the only one who had my number.

Where the hell are you? Big brother was light on words and big on drama.

I cleared the jetway and texted back. *It takes time to put my rod back in my pants. I'll be out in a few minutes.*

A few minutes too soon. I was in no hurry to get to Fury. My life was turning into a murky shade of shit; returning to Fury wasn't my first choice, but it was my only choice. Until the medical board reached a decision, I was in limbo.

I grabbed my bag and walked down the corridor.

"Thank you for your service," an older couple said.

I wasn't surprised that they'd pegged me as military, with my army green duffle, crew cut, and the angry agitation that never left my eyes. It didn't bother me though.

"My pleasure to serve," I replied. I meant every word of it. I'd done eight years in the Army and was planning on another, no matter what Ryker said.

I cleared security and there he was, big and beautiful. As beautiful as any man with a chip the size of a tank on his shoulder could be. He was my brother. He was family. That meant everything to me.

"Hey, Rooster." Ryker wrapped his arms around me and swung me in a circle. Not much had changed since the last time I saw him. His bulk was still as menacing as before, only now he appeared softer—more approachable. The hardness was gone from his eyes.

"It's been way too long," I said. "I've missed you."

He stepped back and looked me over. "You too, bro. You look amazing."

To the unskilled eye, I was in perfect condition. I knew better; he didn't. "I'm good," I lied.

Ryker pulled my duffle from my hands and hoisted it over his back. "You carry this shit everywhere?" He leaned forward, forcing the duffle high on his shoulders.

"My rucksack weighs more." I grabbed my bag back and hefted it onto my shoulder. "You're getting soft in your old age." I was getting soft too. The weight of the sack was nothing as long as I didn't have to run with it or walk too far. That was part of the reason I was stateside.

"I'll show you soft when I get you back to the garage and kick your ass."

My gut burned. "Not sure I'm ready to face Fury sober."

"We're staying in town tonight." Although the nod was slight, the acknowledgment was large.

Getting me to Colorado had been a big undertaking. Getting me back to Fury would take large quantities of alcohol.

We stepped into the cold parking structure. My breath turned to fog on each exhale. And every inhale made my lungs feel like tightened fists.

Ryker clicked his key fob, and the lights flashed on an old blue Subaru.

"That's yours?" He wasn't even a dad yet, but he had the sedan. "Next you'll be trading that shit in for a minivan."

"Man, don't emasculate me more. You already made me sell Dad's bike. Don't saddle me with the minivan."

I tossed my bag in the back and climbed into the shotgun seat. Ryker and I always fought over the front seat as kids. He was older and bigger, and he often won.

Fifteen minutes later, he pulled into the parking lot of a motel. It looked decent. And without any drunks sleeping in front of the doors, it was an upgrade from the barracks in Afghanistan.

Liquor might be banned there, but men got their drink on by making it, smuggling it, or buying it on the black market. One guy's girlfriend filled lotion and shampoo bottles with whiskey. It tasted like soapy shit, but the taste wasn't what the troops were after. It was that moment of bliss where the alcohol took over, and nothing seemed insurmountable.

Hell, I needed a moment of bliss right now. "Let's get a beer and catch up." I reached for the dog tags hanging from my neck and rubbed the cold metal between my thumb and fingers. They represented the regimented life that comforted me.

After we checked in and dropped off our stuff in the room, we walked straight into a nearby bar called the Empty Keg. God help me if the name was accurate. I needed a full keg of bubbly brew and a bottle of whiskey.

Ryker slapped a twenty on the bar. "Two boilermakers."

The grizzled bartender spilled the foam over the mugs, and I damn near drooled. What a beautiful damn sight. "Here's to family." I raised my shot glass.

"Here's to having you home," Ryker said.

We tapped glasses, and I slammed back the shot. The burn ran all the way through my chest and curdled in my stomach.

"You know I'm just back for leave, right?" I sucked in the suds until I got to the cold beer, and then I took a long draw.

"Come on, man. You can't run forever." He stared at me over the rim of the mug.

"There's nothing for me in Fury."

Ryker flinched. My words had hurt him. "Fine, but don't be asking me to sell anything else to help find Decker."

"I want our family back together." My voice was firm and no-nonsense. The type of voice that sent privates scurrying for cover.

Not Ryker. He was like a stone pillar. "What's your end game? You want to find him and then see him once every eight or ten years like you do me? Not happening." He slammed his beer on the bar. "You said my son or daughter would need their uncle. Did you change your mind?"

Nothing in my life was easy, including this conversation. I'd lost my parents, I'd lost my brothers, and now I'd lost my way. Hadn't I lost enough? I didn't want to be a perpetual victim of Fury. There were too many bad memories there. There were too many bad memories everywhere. How did I justify what I wanted when Ryker was right?

"Hey, handsome." A tight little blonde sliding next to me saved me from further interrogation. She smelled like cigarettes and cheap perfume, but she was pretty. After spending year after year in the desert, I wasn't picky. Breathing earned a girl a five. Six if she had teeth, and seven if she bathed. Talking dirty got her an eight; giving head, a nine. Ding ding ding, she'd get a whopping ten if she got dressed and left before I woke up.

This one was currently a seven. "What's up?"

Blondie trailed her too-long, too-fake nail down my chest. "New in town?"

Ryker laughed. "Boy ain't new anywhere." He took off to the head before I could give him a scowl.

"You know every guy who comes to this bar?" I was in Denver, for Christ's sake. Over half a million people lived here.

"I know a few." The chick kept looking over my shoulder, and I knew that look, and I didn't want any trouble. I followed her gaze. The bathroom door opened, but Ryker didn't walk out.

Lumberjack dude's gaze zeroed in on me, or maybe the woman next to me. His pace picked up, and he seemed to grow larger as he got closer.

"Get the hell away from my woman."

I glanced at the blonde. If the smile on her face was any indication, she was pleased with the man's possessiveness.

"You might want to put a leash on her and keep her next to you." I turned and faced the bar. The weathered old man behind it backed away.

"Get the hell away from him." Lumberjack grabbed the blonde's hair and tugged.

She fell on her ass.

"Damnit." I pulled myself off the stool. I hated men who thought they could rule the world with fists and bad attitudes. Being stupid was never a reason to be beaten—unless of course, you were this douchebag. He was begging to be beat.

I pushed him away from her, which pissed him off more. The first punch was a doozy, but I'd felt worse, and I was ready for some fist action.

My right would have been too powerful for this asshole, so I gave him a left jab that sent him stumbling backward. The thing about big men was they fell hard. Bigger didn't make you better. Bigger made you a better target.

The woman screeched, "Don't let him hit you, Buck!"—ironic, since she put up with his abuse, but he took her advice. A swing and miss from him, followed by a single from me, and the guy fell hard.

"Stay down, you big idiot." Idiot was right. Buck might have had bulk, but he was lacking in brains. He came at me again.

I let the fury loose. I gave him my right, and my next punch flattened the asshole. But the shit I'd bottled for years and the adrenaline flooding my veins didn't relent. Fist ready and legs braced, I was ready for all takers. I was ready when the big idiot tried to rise again. An uppercut and the guy was down, but I wasn't done. Fist mid-flight, I aimed for the kidney.

"What the hell, Silas? You're going to kill him!" Ryker yelled.

My fist froze midair. My knuckles dripped blood. My whole body vibrated with the need to release the hit on the prone man, a broken man, a man blanketed by the blonde who'd played her game at both our expenses.

"Why should this idiot live when better people die?" I never understood why one man died and another lived.

"You don't get to choose." Ryker grabbed my elbow and pulled me to the bar.

I turned away. "If I did, my life would have been different." *Yep, all of our lives would have been different.*

CHAPTER 3

GRACE

I stood in the living room and rocked Blue, sang to Blue, bounced Blue in the football hold that normally comforted him. Tonight, nothing worked. He'd already cried and howled and refused my tit and showed no signs of ending his fit of tears.

I paced back and forth and swung him side to side to side. Might have been the day of shopping or the iced tea. Could have been that I was tired and cross and grumpy too. Basically, breastfeeding moms were supposed to eat cardboard and stay perfectly peaceful to keep their babies happy. Too bad I was human.

I cradled him and rocked him and patted him until he burped. I bathed him and bounced him, hoping he'd tire, needing him to go to sleep. Blue wouldn't cave. He was the man of the hour, and probably the next hour too.

Screaming baby on my shoulder and exhaustion in every bone of my body, I collapsed on the couch and scrolled through the channels until I found American Movie Classics. Romance was bullshit, but I loved the old-time love stories like *The African Queen, Breakfast at Tiffany's, It Happened One Night*. I rubbed my once-flat stomach and thought about a lot of nights when it happened. Afternoons, too, in his office.

Blue squirmed against my shoulder, and I slid him down to his favorite spot, my breast. "Typical man." I kissed my son's fuzzy melon. "But the thing about older movies, Blue, is that back then, men did the right thing." I tried to explain the way of the world to an infant. "Instead of throwing a few hundred bucks at a pregnant girl and telling her to take care of it, they stuck it out or at least helped support them."

Blue's face scrunched up at my take on life, or my movie choice, or the refried beans I'd scarfed while he suckled. Note to self: no more Mexican food.

The theme song for *My Fair Lady* tinkled out of the tube, and I leaned back into the sofa. Blue's face turned red, and I turned up the volume. I was surely in for another doozy of a fit. Generally, he was a good baby. But when I was a less-than-stellar mother, we both suffered. "I suck as a mother. I'm so sorry, sweetheart, but I needed those enchiladas and rice and beans and the salsa ... well, I didn't need that, but it was good."

He let out a wail that could be heard in Boulder.

I dragged myself to my feet and zigzagged past the tan sofa to the red chair to the old walnut desk that Mona had given me. She'd said she couldn't see well enough to use it, and there weren't any men waiting to bend her over it, so she might as well get rid of it. Sadly, the only man in my life was the one in my arms who refused to give in to sleep.

"Please, baby, just sleep," I crooned until my voice went hoarse. I rocked until my arms went numb and paced until I couldn't feel my feet, but finally, mercifully, thanks to the goddess of all mothers, Blue's cries softened. His eyes drooped. "Thank you. Thank you," I whispered.

And then the doorbell rang.

Blue jolted back to nuclear level.

"Damnit all to hell." I grabbed the knob, wanting to scream, and cry, and tell the only old man who'd dare bother me at this time to leave me alone. Hell, I wanted to pretend I wasn't home, but with the decibels Blue put out, there was no way to pretend.

Mr. Chambers stood on my porch, tapping his cane.

"I'm sorry, Mr. Chambers. Blue seems to have a bit of gas tonight." I cradled my son to my chest, and his screams notched down to short bursts of unhappiness and hiccups.

"Can't you shut him up?" The old duffer tapped his cane against the cracked concrete.

The devil on my right shoulder wanted the tip of his cane to stick so he'd stumble backward and leave. But the left angel always took pity. The man had to be like one hundred and twenty-six years old ... okay, more like eighty.

"Look, he's calming down. If you'd lower your voice, I'm sure I can get him to sleep."

"How nice for him. What about me?" His cane tapped harder.

"You want me to breastfeed and rock you too?" I was tired. Tired of being lonely. Tired of being tired. And tired of this old fart knocking on my door each time Blue made a peep.

"Young people." He shook his cane. "You have more lip than sense."

I didn't back down. As weak and old and tired as he was, if he went for a hit, only my ankles would be at risk.

"You may be right. If I'd used my lips, I wouldn't have this beautiful boy that frustrates you so much. I swear, Mr. Chambers, you whine more than he does."

The damn man either had supersonic hearing or was a stalker, standing outside my window and waiting for the first sound to happen so he could complain. Or it could have been that the houses were built with papier-mâché and string. Yep, the insulation was thin, which meant the soundproofing was shit.

"You know, if you'd done it right, you'd have a man here to help you out."

I covered Blue's exposed ear with my hand. "Oh, a man helped get me here." I leaned toward the old coot and burned him with my laser glare. "The problem with men is, they want everything, and when they get it, they complain. What about you, Mr. Chambers, did you hold your wife's hand while she pushed a bowling ball out of her vagina? Did you get up for 2, 4, and 6 A.M. feedings? Did you?" My voice grew until it hit Blue's full-on-tilt level. "Or did you sit on your lazy ass and tell your wife to shut that kid up?"

His expression twisted, and his chin quivered. "I'm an old man, and I don't need this stress."

I huffed out a groan. "You're like my father, always ready to offer advice but never a hand. Go home, Mr. Chambers, and eat your strained peas, fart in your lounger, and stop judging me every second of the day." I slammed the door in his face. My left angel tut-tut-tutted, but righty groaned. She was still as cranky as her quieting son.

Blue jolted awake with a blood-curdling scream.

I sank to the floor, joined Blue in a fit of tears and texted Ana.

SOS!

I'd never considered being mean to an old man before. Maybe Mexican food didn't agree with me either.

No more than five minutes later, Ana used her key to let herself in. Her ability to magically appear when needed was the greatest part of living on the same street as my best friend.

The worst part was constantly seeing her happy when I was so miserable and lonely and needed a man.

"It's okay, darling." She slipped Blue from my hands. "I got him."

"Thank you," I cried. I was so grateful for her presence; I'd never felt so lonely. Infants didn't make good conversationalists, as it turned out. They made stretch marks and sagging boobs.

"What happened?" Ana put Blue in a football hold. All it took was a few laps around the living room, and he was out.

"Mr. Chambers yelled at us."

"What's wrong with that man? Blue's a baby. Babies cry." She took a final lap around the living room and walked Blue down the hallway to his bedroom. When she returned, I was in the kitchen making decaffeinated tea.

"Remind me not to drink iced tea or eat stuff that my son won't like."

Ana shrugged. "You never listen." She reached into the cupboard and pulled out the sugar. "Tell me what's bothering you."

"I'm not sure." That wasn't the truth. There were a lot of things bothering me, from the lack of passion in my life to my sore nipples.

"I think Blue is feeding off your anxiety."

That I could be the reason for my son's distress tore at my insides. "You're probably right." I couldn't pinpoint the culprit exactly, but it was a bunch of things all rolled into one. "My life is not like I imagined."

Ana took her cup of chamomile tea and went back into the living room.

"And whose is? Stop being such a twat. You've got an amazing son. A great house. You've managed to find a way to support both of you by working from home, and you have me as a friend. That alone should make you happy." Ana blew on her tea, the steam rising past her bangs.

"I know I'm lucky. The problem is, I'm lonely. You never needed a man in your life, but you got Ryker. And he's an amazing man and will be an awesome father. I have no one but you two and Nate and Mona, and none of you are warming my bed."

"You're a single mother. It's not like your vagina fell off when you gave birth." She moved to the couch and snuggled up next to me. Her eyes grew as big as baseballs. "It didn't, did it?" She rubbed her rounded belly.

I laughed. "No. I mean, I haven't used it since I got pregnant, but it seems fine."

"Okay then." She let out a sigh. "You need to put yourself out there."

"Out there?" I rolled my eyes. "I had a baby, and I'm nowhere near married. I think I was way out there already."

"You know what I mean. You haven't been attracted to the right men. You're always after … I don't know, if they're not peacocks, then they're jerks."

I shrugged. "You know what they say. A girl falls for men like her father."

Ana shook her head, and Blue started crying again. She rose from her seat before I could muster the energy to move. "I'll check on him. You stay here."

When she left the room, I looked down at my vibrating cell and sighed. Another call from Dad. I powered the phone down, not ready to be judged by another man tonight.

CHAPTER 4

GRACE

Ana slid into the diner booth across from me. "Are you doing better today?"

"You were a godsend. Thank you." After she'd left last night, I crashed while Blue slept for almost six hours straight. "What the heck is it about your football hold that gets him to settle so nicely?"

"It's not the hold, he just loves his Aunt Ana." She waved to Hannah, but the waitress gave us a disinterested glance and turned her back. "So, I stayed up last night thinking about your dilemma." She pulled two packets of sugar from the container and set them in front of her.

"What dilemma?"

Ana rolled her eyes and let out a huff. "Your loneliness."

"Forget I said anything." I looked down at Blue, lying in his carrier. Sound asleep, he was absolutely beautiful. His eyelashes were so long they rested on his cheek, and I knew I'd be beating the girls off with a stick when he grew up. "Can you imagine what my life would be like if I had to use what time I did have to stroke some guy's ego? I'm better off alone."

Ana laughed. "It's not his ego you'd be stroking."

"You did not say that." I looked at my best friend and rose from the booth. "Watch him." I was tired of waiting for Hannah. She was still pissed at Ana for winning Ryker when she never could, but I didn't deserve to be ignored. Besides, I was hungry.

I stomped toward the counter where Hannah stood eating a piece of pie. "Think we could get some menus and decaf coffee?"

She slid her half-eaten plate onto the back counter and turned toward me. "Oh, I'm sorry." She smiled that knife-in-the-back, passive-aggressive way... "I didn't see you come in."

"Now you see we're here." I could give as good as I got, and my tone was sharp enough to Ginzu right through her smarmy attitude. "Decaf, please."

I rejoined Ana and Blue, and Hannah followed. As she slapped the menus on the table and sloshed decaf into our cups, I bit my tongue. I didn't want her spitting in my food.

"And what can I get you to eat?" Hannah tapped her pen as Ana and I took our time perusing the menus we surely knew by heart. Two—or three—could play the passive-aggressive game.

Ana ordered pancakes and bacon, and I an egg white omelet, but I topped it off with a genuine smile. Hannah had the means and motive to poison our food. Ana would be her first hit because she had Ryker, but I'd be a close second because I had Ana.

When Hannah finally left, Ana leaned across the table. "What about Nate?"

"What about him?" But I knew what she was getting at. "Nate and I flirted for a while but fizzled."

"Maybe you should revisit that option. I know he likes you."

"Nate's no Ryker." Sure, he was an awesome guy, but he wasn't *my* guy. The problem was, he didn't make my lady bits tingle. "If Nate and Ryker were cuts of beef, Nate would be choice while Ryker would be prime."

Ana blushed to cherry red. "Ryker *is* pretty prime."

Hannah slammed the food onto the table. "Your relationship is a fad." She was young but full of bitterness beyond her years.

Ana rubbed her stomach. "He's a pretty amazing fad, then."

Hannah narrowed her eyes at Ana's baby bump and stomped away.

My phone vibrated across the table. I looked at the lit-up screen. It was my father again. I grabbed the phone and quickly sent him a text: *Can't answer right now. I'll call you later.*

It wasn't a lie. I'd call him later. It might be a year from now, or maybe when Blue graduated from college, but someday I'd call.

"You have to tell him." Ana squirted a mountain of ketchup on her hash browns. "It's not fair that he has a grandson floating around in the world that he doesn't know about."

"Do you know what he'd do if he found out about Blue? He wouldn't be mad that I didn't tell him." I reached inside to my inner actress and pulled out the snarky girl. "Oh, no, he'd be darn right proud that his only kid got knocked up and isn't married. Don't forget he's a fire-and-brimstone deacon. He'd disown me after he took his belt to me. He'd—"

I shook my head and forked up a heap of omelet, the food stopping any further description. That meeting wouldn't be pleasant. Surely Blue could handle that once, but he couldn't and didn't need to handle a lifetime of my father. I didn't want his kind of abuse around us. I'd had enough of men who demanded and controlled. Men who walked away.

We sat and ate in silence. I picked at my food while Ana cleaned her plate. She looked out the window and pulled her napkin to her ashen face.

"What is it?" I reached for her. "Are you okay?" I knew she shouldn't eat ketchup like an entrée.

"I think I know why your father has been calling you so much lately." Ana pointed out the window.

The omelet spun in my stomach, and my muscles tightened in preparation to cower—the sign to grab my son and run. My father stood outside the diner. "Oh, my God. Hide." I slunk down as far as I could. Any farther and my face would be in my half-eaten breakfast. I raised my eyes to Ana. "Is he still standing there? Does he see us?"

Ana melted into the red leather seat across from me. "He's looking at a map," she whispered like a CIA operative. "Why the hell is he here?"

Of course, Blue picked this time to wake up. He wasn't crying, he was cooing, but I couldn't hide under the table for long. My little man would want attention.

"You have to go out there," Ana whispered. "Find out why he's here. I can pretend Blue is mine until you're ready to tell him."

I laid my hand on Blue's stomach. "I won't deny my son." My voice had more strength than my legs. "Besides, you're pregnant right now. There's no way he'd think you just had a newborn."

"You're right."

"Damnit." I pulled myself back into the booth. I couldn't put it off any longer. I couldn't hide in the diner all day. I couldn't live in fear of being found out. It was time to come clean.

I stood up and pulled Blue from his carrier. With him pressed to my chest, I walked outside to face the fiddler. "Hey, Dad."

"Oh, Grace." He pivoted and froze. His eyes went from mine to the baby and back.

I raised my chin. I hadn't seen him in over a year. He hadn't approved of my old lifestyle. He hadn't approved of my job. Hell, he'd never approved of me.

"Is this why you're hiding?" His face turned crimson red. "Your mother will be furious."

Bringing up my mother was the worst thing he could've done. They didn't even live together. I was pretty sure they rarely talked.

"Is she enjoying Aspen?"

"Does she know about this?" He pointed his sausage-like finger at my son.

"He's not a *this*. His name is Blue. And I haven't told her." I hugged my son closer to my breast.

"You didn't tell anyone. What are you hiding, Grace? Who's the father?"

"No one you know."

"Trapped him into it, huh?" Tension slid from my father's face, and his tight expression softened a smidgen. "All right, then," he said, seemingly appeased. "At least you did the right thing by your child. A child needs a father, and you need a husband." He stepped to the side to see Blue, who had fallen back asleep in my arms. "I can't wait to meet this husband of yours."

I was talented, but I couldn't create a husband out of nothing. "About that..."

He crumpled up the map in his hand. "There was a wedding, wasn't there, Grace? Tell me there was a wedding!"

Old fear welled up inside and forced me to lie. "Of course, there was a wedding." I was going straight to hell for lots of stuff if my father was right. Premarital sex. Not going to church. Using birth control. Might as well add lying to it. "It was all of a sudden. That's all."

"I got an email saying you moved to Fury, and then nothing for months. Ten months, Grace, and you had a wedding? One I didn't get invited to? What will my parish think if they find out that you, my only child, didn't ask your father to officiate?"

"I don't care what they think. I'm not the girl you tell everyone at church I am. I can't be part of your made-up world. Even Mom left you years ago because she was tired of perpetuating your lies. Perfection doesn't exist."

"Your mom left Denver because—" He waved the wrinkled map in his hand like he was swatting at flies.

"Not because the pollution was bad," I said, "but because her life with you was polluted."

"Don't you talk about my marriage when you didn't even invite me to yours. I want to meet this man you call husband."

CHAPTER 5

SILAS

The silence in the car was deafening. Ryker hadn't said a word to me since the bar fight last night. In fact, after Buck had hit the ground like a felled tree, he'd turned and walked out. I'd stayed to drink myself numb.

Finally, Ryker broke literal hours of silence. "Are you ready to talk about last night?" His voice was calm, his gaze steady on the road.

"There's nothing to talk about." I looked out the window. The forest thickened as we entered the pass between Boulder and Fury. My lungs felt heavy like they were filling with fluid. They weren't, of course; it was old memories weighing me down.

"Seriously, dude, you almost killed that guy."

I glanced at Ryker. His jaw was tight, and in that moment, he reminded me of our father, Raptor. Thank God, he wasn't Dad because I wouldn't be sitting on my ass right now. In fact, I wouldn't be sitting on my ass for a week. Raptor Savage didn't put up with much, and he surely never asked a question twice.

"He deserved what he got," I said as if that was answer enough.

"What the hell did he do?"

"He was a bully." I stared back out the window. Somehow with the miles that had passed, I'd reverted back to my six-year-old self—the boy who had lost everything because of the actions of an asshole.

"Lots of people are assholes." He made a left turn onto a two-lane highway. "You gonna beat the shit out of all of them?"

We were on the last leg of the trip.

"What happened to you? You were the smartest of us. The best. You wouldn't hurt anyone."

"That was before." I leaned my head against the cool window, hoping it would calm the heat building inside me.

"Before what?"

"Before I realized life isn't fair, and that sometimes assholes finish first."

"Not that asshole."

"Nope, the poor sucker barely got started." I thought about the way he pulled the blonde by the hair and tossed her to the ground like she didn't matter. That had pissed me off. It still pissed me off. In truth, the only time I adopted the asshole persona was to best an asshole. I reached over and cranked up the radio. As far as I was concerned, the subject was closed.

Twenty minutes later, we passed by the sign that read, "Welcome to Fury." It was the same sign that was there twenty years ago. Only back then it seemed so much bigger.

"This place looks the same." My tone dripped with disgust, and a knot the size of a Harley sat in my chest.

"If you stick around for more than a day, you might realize it's not. I've been working on the house above the garage. I figured since you're back, we can work on it together, and you can stay there now that I'm living with Ana."

"If that's what gets you off."

Ryker bristled. "What the hell is going on with you? You weren't like this over Skype. You were happy. What happened?"

"Maybe it's because I wasn't here," I snapped back. "This place has never brought me anything but agony."

I thought we were heading for the garage, but at the last second Ryker whipped the car into the diner parking lot.

"What are we doing here?" Not even the diner had changed much. Same big red flashing arrow, pointing at the same dirty, whitewashed building.

"Ana's here." He pointed toward a beat-up black Jeep.

The only good thing about coming to Fury was meeting Ana. To be honest, I'd met her when we were kids, but I'd known her as Sparrow. It was funny how things changed and yet remained the same. I'd always felt like the massacre was my fault because Ryker had told me to watch Sparrow and Decker. When she'd run off, I'd had to decide, and I'd chosen to stay with my baby brother.

The death of Sparrow had ruined Ryker and me. His guilt manifested into anger. Mine manifested into something completely different. For years, I believed every dreadful thing that happened to me was payback for her life and the lives of the dozens who died that day. Now I knew differently, and that knowledge filled me with emotions I wasn't ready to deal with.

I followed Ryker to the front of the diner where a hot redhead was standing next to a man twice her age. I stopped to take a better look at the pair. She could do better than him for sure. It was a second later that I saw the baby, and an ache settled in my stomach until the woman looked up. Her smile was the kind that could light a dark day.

"There you are." She came at me like I was an old friend, and I would have backed off, asked what was going on, but those jade eyes and that wicked grin … "I've been waiting for you." She stretched up onto her tiptoes and whispered in my ear, "Go with it." And then she covered my mouth with her lips in the sweetest kiss.

CHAPTER 6

GRACE

Oh. My. God. I kissed a stranger. A sexy stranger who could kiss like a porn star, or at least how I imagined a porn star would kiss. I mean, they'd have to be good at it since they do it all the time.

So now I'd not only lied but also basically accosted a stranger. Talk about inserting my foot in my mouth. Right then I would've liked to insert it straight up my own ass.

I couldn't help myself. When I saw Ryker and the brother he was always talking about step out of the car—as gorgeous as I had ever imagined—I acted without thought. I figured that since Ryker was always telling me what good a guy his brother was, maybe he'd help me out, albeit in an unconventional way.

"Dad." I hugged Blue closer to my chest with one hand and wrapped my hand through Silas's arm. We moved toward my father, and I prayed that he'd play along for a few more minutes. "This is Silas … my husband."

Silas tensed, but he didn't out me. He simply smiled and offered his free hand to shake. "Nice to meet you, sir."

Oh, he was good. I'd owe him big-time for this award-winning performance.

My dad looked Silas up and down as if he was gauging his worth.

Narcissistic parents like my father assessed everyone's value by a personal comparison. As long as they fell above the average but below the parent, they would be accepted.

I watched my father take in everything about the man in front of him. His eyes went from his black biker boots to the knit cap on his head embroidered with the word *Army*. I relished the moment too because, like my father, I wasn't immune to Silas Savage. He was gorgeous, and looking at him was a treat.

"An Army man." Dad pumped Silas's hand in a strong shake, and when I saw my father wince from the grip Silas had, I felt a surge of pride swell in my chest. It was crazy because I had no claim on Silas, but he was helping me, and for the moment, he was mine.

"Yes, sir. Eight years." Silas looked over at me, and a light twinkled in his eyes. "Your daughter is the only thing that keeps me going when I'm deployed."

He wrapped his arm around my waist but let it fall to my ass. "Ah, that's so sweet."

His lips pressed against mine, and I longed to prolong the kiss. To turn it into something more than what it was. "You know it's true, honey." He emphasized the word *honey* for my father's benefit.

Silas slid his hand into my back pocket and gripped a handful of my ass. I stepped aside and swatted him away. "So, Dad, why are you here?"

"I've got some business here for the church. Besides, I wanted to check on you, and I'm darn glad I did so I could find out I've got a son-in-law and a grandson."

Finally, my dad took a close look at Blue and said, "He's a handsome one, isn't he?"

Silas looked down at my son with softness in his expression. "I wasn't here for his birth. You know, I was in the desert, but my sweetness here was a real trooper."

My dad looked at Silas and asked, "What's his name again?"

Silas didn't miss a beat. "To me, he's my buddy." He pulled the sleeping baby from me and cradled him in his arms.

"I told you, Dad, his name is Blue."

"That's right, Blue," Silas confirmed like he named the baby himself.

"Son, I'm happy my daughter chose a soldier," my dad said. "I couldn't be prouder if you were my own son, but don't think you're getting away with anything here. I know what's going on."

I held my breath, terrified that my father had figured out the ruse. I couldn't see how as Silas played his part so well. He was pretty damn good for stepping in without a script.

In perfect soldier fashion, Silas stood staring at my dad. "What do you mean, sir?"

To my surprise, he slapped Silas on the back. "We need to talk about your time in the desert. I know what you're thinking—an old deacon like myself wouldn't know anything about war—but you'd be wrong. I offer counsel to a lot of our boys coming back from war."

"A deacon?"

"Grace didn't tell you?"

Silas turned toward me. "No, Grace didn't say a thing." He said my name like it was a delicacy, and my insides churned.

My father laid his hand on Blue's head like he was blessing him. "She's not forthcoming when it comes to religion, so that doesn't surprise me. What about you, son? Do you believe in God?"

"Dad, Silas recently got back from deployment. You're not allowed to interrogate him."

My father looked at the two of us, and a sly smile crossed his face. "I get it. You've been gone a while. Get him home, Grace, and take care of your man."

It would be so easy to reach up and slap my dad. It was that disgusting belief that women were meant to serve that ate my mother alive until there was nothing left to give, driving her to leave. But when she left, she left everything. Me included.

"I have to check into my room anyway, but I insist on meeting you both for dinner tomorrow. Outside of town there's a steakhouse called Tripp's. Let's meet there at seven."

He turned and walked away without waiting for our confirmation. That was Dad. He expected obedience. He didn't give any consideration to the fact that my fake husband had come home from a war zone. He didn't seem to notice—or care—that my real son had a schedule. Babies went to bed early. Well, not Blue. He made sure to keep Mr. Chambers up for a while before he gave in to sleep. But that wasn't the point. The point was that Dad only considered himself.

As soon as my dad was out of earshot, I turned to Silas. "Thank you so much. I owe you."

"You're welcome." He looked me over like I was a chocolate éclair. "I'm going to demand payment."

Of course, he was. I'd never known a man that did something for nothing. That wasn't completely true because Ryker did things all the time for everyone. Meanwhile, Mona was always kind to me, but she expected me to entertain her with stories about naked men and oral sex. That woman had been born in the wrong century.

What I meant was that I hadn't had the experience of a man doing something out of the kindness of his heart.

"I'm Grace, by the way."

"I got that much. You must be Ana's friend, Grace"

"Yep, that's me."

Silas shifted Blue into one arm. My already ten-pound son was dwarfed by his thick arms. "And this is our son, Blue." He looked down at him, clearly admiring the little guy, and my heart swelled with pride.

One thing I was sure of: My son was the prettiest baby on the planet.

"Thanks for playing along. It's a long story."

"I can't wait to hear it." He wrapped his free hand around my waist and led me toward the front door of the diner. "You know what's funny, Grace? I don't remember us together, and that's a shame because I swear I'd remember a girl like you. And look at my son. He's got my eyes, don't you think?"

I laughed. "That he does, honey." I mimicked his inflection from earlier.

Silas still held Blue, who was now awake staring up at him. "How'd he get the name Blue?"

"That's another story for another day."

"Mrs. Savage, it sounds like we have a lot of catching up to do."

My breath hitched at the sound of that. Mrs. Savage. It sounded so appealing to be a Mrs. in general. Years ago, I would have said that a woman didn't need a man, and I'd still stick to that statement. But sometimes a woman wanted a man, and something told me I was going to want Silas Savage more than I should.

He wasn't my type. He wasn't refined. He didn't wear a suit. He didn't work nine to five. He probably didn't have much of a savings account if he was anything like Ryker.

Ana always said I had a thing for peacocks—men who strutted their beautiful faces and accomplishments—but Silas wasn't anything like those men. No, Silas wasn't a peacock. He was a rooster, and all I could think about after that kiss was he was the nicest cock I'd met in a long time.

CHAPTER 7

SILAS

That Grace girl was cute, and she sure could kiss. The baby had thrown me for a loop, but what the hell? I opened the door and followed her into the diner. *Nice ass.*

"Glad you two could join us," Ryker said, pointing to the bench across from him and Ana.

I smiled lazily at the former Sparrow. "So, this is your bun oven." Ryker's eyes opened wide. I knew that comment would get to him, but I wanted to see what it would do to her.

She leaned into Ryker's shoulder. "You want to kick his ass, or should I?"

"Dude, you don't meet the mother of your niece or nephew and call her a bun oven." Ryker reached over and grabbed a piece of uneaten bacon from Ana's plate.

Grace took Blue from my arms and put him in a baby seat at the end of the red leather bench.

I leaned over and gave Ana a kiss on the cheek. "You sure did grow up pretty. I remember when you were a scrawny little rat, stomping your light-up shoes." I backed up and slid into the booth next to Grace.

"I loved those shoes. Even when I lived with Grams, I wore those light-up shoes." Ana looked toward the red-headed beauty who sat next to me. "I see you've met Grace."

"Oh, you mean my wife, Grace." I looked past her to the car seat that had a monkey-shaped rattle hanging from the handle. Blue's big eyes were zeroed in on the toy. "And apparently I have a son."

Ana bolted upright. "You didn't."

Grace sunk into the seat. "I didn't have much choice. Dad started going on about a wedding. He was winding up for his you're-an-awful-daughter diatribe. I didn't want to hear him try to convince me that Blue was a bad decision, so I blurted out that I had a husband." She shrugged her shoulders. "Then Ryker and Silas showed up, and it kind of took on its own life."

I was getting ready to razz Grace when a cute blonde waitress rushed over. "Hi, you must be Silas." She sat down next to me on the edge of the booth and scooted her ass into my hip, which forced me to move closer to Grace.

"I am Silas." I looked over at Ryker, who was shaking his head. It dawned on me right then that this was the waitress Nate told me about. The one who had it bad for Ryker. "You must be Hannah."

The girl bloomed right next to me. "I am, sweetie. What can I get you?" She leaned toward me, making sure her body rubbed against mine.

I looked around the table and noticed a barely eaten omelet. "Whose is this?"

"That was mine before I lost my appetite," Grace said.

"You finished?" I asked, even as I reached for the plate.

"Go for it, sweetie." Grace did a perfect impression of happy Hannah.

"Thanks, peaches." I leaned toward Grace to get her fork and brushed my lips over her cheek. I leaned back and sent Hannah falling from the booth onto her butt.

"You, too?" she demanded.

I had no idea what she meant, and I didn't care. "Yes, two coffees." I looked at Ryker, Ana, and Grace. "You guys want anything?"

Ryker ordered a patty melt while Grace and Ana ordered decaffeinated coffee. Hannah stomped off while I cut through the cold eggs and relished the texture as it hit my tongue. Even cold eggs beat the MREs I ate in the field.

Blue worked himself up to a mini-fit, and Grace pulled him out of the carrier. "Do you mind?" She looked around the booth.

Everyone shook their heads. Grace covered her shoulder with a light green blanket and tucked Blue beneath it. Ryker and Ana couldn't see a thing, but I got a regular peep show as she maneuvered her beautiful breast out of her shirt and into the baby's mouth. It was a total jerk move to stare at her, but I couldn't help myself. Any man would have done the same. My species couldn't turn away from a nice set of breasts. I would have done anything to trade places with that kid.

Once Grace had Blue settled and happy, she turned her upper body toward me, taking away my peek at her perfection.

"I'm sorry to bring you into my mess, Silas."

Ryker broke into uncontrolled laughter. "I wish I had been standing there when you told your dad that Silas was your man."

Ana laughed too. "I would have loved to see both of their faces. Deacon Faraday's face, just to get smug satisfaction from the fact that he was wrong about Grace. And you, Silas. What did your face look like when she approached you? I saw her pull you in and kiss you. I had no idea what the hell was going on."

Hannah brought Ryker's meal and the decaf coffee pot. I reached for Grace's cold coffee and washed down the egg before Hannah filled her cup. "I don't put up much of a fuss when a beautiful woman wants to kiss me," I laughed. Hannah rolled her eyes before she walked away.

Out of the corner of my eye, I saw Grace smile. Her whole face lit up.

"He was a trooper," she said. "He didn't even flinch. The problem I have now is that my dad is in town for a few days on church business. He wants to have dinner with my husband and me tomorrow night." She tucked her chin into the blanket, and her smile fell. "I'll come clean tomorrow at dinner."

Ryker piped in, "Or maybe Silas can finish the job. He can be your baby daddy until your dad leaves."

My facial muscles twitched in sync, and Grace came to the rescue. "Don't worry about dinner. I'll tell him the truth. Not that it'll be easy at this point, but I'll handle it."

It was a shame to see that bright smile turn into something that looked like worry.

She removed Blue from her breast with a pop and latched him on to her other side. I was once again given a titillating view of her tatas. I was even more jealous of the little man. To be pressed to those breasts several times a day would be heaven.

"I have to say, bro, Blue looked good in your arms."

"That's never going to happen." I looked at the boy who was now flopped on his mother's shoulder while she patted his back. He was cute enough, and I liked the way he felt in my arms, but I was soldier material, not father material. "I mean, the kid is cute and all, but I don't see myself ever becoming a father. Not after what our foster dad did."

Grace nodded, and her whole demeanor changed. She wilted like an out-of-water flower.

I pulled a twenty from my wallet and slapped it on the table. "Ryker, are you going to show me around the booming metropolis of Fury?"

"What? At the mention of responsibility and parenting, you want to bail?"

He was right. It was a subject that bothered me. I'd never thought about settling down before. But seeing Ryker with Ana each time we Skyped and now seeing him sit beside her completely content made me wonder if he didn't have something amazing started. There was a tiny, twisted knot of jealousy forming in my gut.

"We can stay, but you mentioned working on the house, so I figured we could get started right away."

"Let me finish eating. We have to hit Mona's first. She'd never forgive me if I didn't bring you by her place." Ryker picked up his patty melt and consumed it in six bites. He drank his coffee and leaned over to give Ana a kiss. "I'll see you soon."

I looked at Grace, who was getting Blue ready to leave. It would have been so easy to lean down and kiss her again. I wanted to feel and taste her lips once more, but that wasn't wise. Grace was the kind of woman who needed a full-time man. Blue needed a full-time father. *Full* wasn't a word synonymous with Silas Savage unless you were saying he was full of shit.

Instead, I said simply, "Nice to meet you, Grace," like we hadn't shared the most amazing kiss.

Fifteen minutes later, we were pulling in to Mona's driveway. She opened the door as soon as we walked up the steps.

"Get in here." She opened the door wide and stepped aside to make room for us to pass. I wondered whether she knew she was wearing one pink sock and one red one. "I don't own the electric company, and it's cold out there." She waited for us to step into her living room, and then she locked the door tight. "I made hot cocoa."

Ryker looked at me and smiled. "You're in for a treat."

We followed her into the small kitchen where hot milk steamed in a pan on the stove. She gave it a quick stir and then stepped back.

"Let me look at you." She walked around me like she was inspecting high-end goods. "I hate winter," she grumbled. "Now take off that coat and beanie so I can see if you're as ripped as your brother."

I let out a mock gasp. Ryker entertained me with Mona's antics each time we spoke. I wrapped my arms around her thick waist and picked her up. "Mona, you're a cougar," I said, mock-scolding, as I turned her in a circle.

She didn't fight all that hard. In fact, her hands went to my arms, and she squeezed like she was testing the ripeness of a peach. "Put me down, young man."

I set her softly on the worn-out linoleum flooring. It was probably original. It still had a harvest gold hue, but the pattern's color had been completely rubbed off in several places, leaving white cloudy dots that clearly marked the high-traffic areas.

I pulled off my jacket and beanie and ran my hands over my recently sheared head. After three days of no shaving, my scruff was almost as long as my hair.

Mona dumped cocoa powder and sugar into the simmering milk. "This here's the secret ingredient." She unwrapped two chocolate bars and broke them into pieces as she added them to the mix. How the nearly blind woman managed to make anything was a mystery to me.

She ladled the steaming mix into three owl mugs and set them on the Formica table. "Okay, young man. I need some answers."

I leaned back and sipped the hot chocolate. I had to give her credit; it was the best I'd ever had. "What do you want to know?" I knew from Ryker that when you spoke to Mona, you used your best diction and grammar skills. She'd be as quick with a correction as she was with her treats.

"Are you here for good, son?" She leaned forward and stared at me like she was a human lie detector, but I knew she was just trying to see me. I didn't know Mona well, but I felt like I knew her through Ryker. He always had a good Mona story to share.

"No, ma'am. I'm on leave waiting on reassignment." That teetered on the truth. I was waiting on the Army, but it wasn't for reassignment. Not exactly.

"Oh, pish. Your brother is going to be a father. You're going to be an uncle. We've got a few single women in town that you could court." She ran her hand through her white curly hair.

"Are you volunteering?" I asked. From what Ryker told me, she could take a good ribbing as easily as she could give it.

"In my heyday, young man, I could have given you a run for your money."

Ryker let loose a laugh. "She'd wear you out, Silas."

"But I'd have a private supply of hot chocolate."

"Oh, lord. Like I told your brother, I'm too old to have your babies, so find yourself a nice young woman and knock her up." She leaned back and enjoyed a sip of her cocoa.

Ryker leaned in like he was going to tell her a secret. "He's married to Grace."

Mona spit out a mouthful of hot chocolate, showering me and Ryker with a sticky mess. "You married her already?" Her light blue eyes grew as big as saucers. "You have good taste. That girl is a keeper."

"We are not married." It seemed like every conversation I'd had since I arrived back in Fury involved me marrying Grace. "Her preacher dad showed up, and I guess she hadn't told him about Blue and … well … I stood in as her husband. We were fake married for five minutes."

Mona twisted her mouth in the way some people did when they were thinking. "You could do a lot worse than Grace. She's beautiful inside and out."

I looked up to the ceiling and rolled my eyes. "Not happening, Mona."

"Good thing. I can't recommend you if you can't speak in full sentences."

I had to laugh—I'd been warned about my language, but I'd still been caught. "So, what you're telling me is I could do worse than Grace, and she could do better than me." I was in love with this old woman. She was exactly whom I would have picked as a grandmother if I'd been given a choice.

And Mona's response only served to convince me further. "That's exactly what I'm saying," she said smugly.

CHAPTER 8

GRACE

"What do you think of Silas?" Ana was finishing her coffee while I buckled Blue into his carrier and covered him with a blanket. It was a sunny, winter day, but it was still cold.

"He's nice enough, but he's not for me." The sad truth was I liked him a lot, but Blue was my priority, and I didn't have time for a man who didn't want kids. Blue and I were a package deal.

"I don't know. He seemed taken with you." Ana wrapped a knit scarf around her neck. Mona must have made it because none of the colors matched. She had made booties for Blue, too. I loved them although—or maybe because—one was navy blue and the other black.

In dire need of a haircut, I pushed the strands that had fallen in my face. Who knew hair grew twice as fast when you were pregnant? "He was taken with my boobs." A flush raced up from my chest to my face as I remembered how he stared at Blue nursing.

"Give him time. It's hard for him to come back here. He's never returned since the massacre. The last time Ryker saw him, they met in a neutral location in Denver."

I couldn't imagine coming back to the place where your life had changed so dramatically. That would be like me moving back home. The thought of that made my stomach lurch.

"Is he staying with you, or is he staying at the house above the garage?" I couldn't imagine him staying at The Nest. Not only was it the place where his parents were murdered, but I also wasn't sure there was anything left in there but dust and cobwebs.

"He's got the couch unless you're offering up half of your bed." She gave me an exaggerated brow waggle and slid from the booth.

"Girl, as nice as that sounds, I'll have to pass." It did sound nice. I'd kissed the man, and that alone was a toe-curling experience. I was pretty sure that tongue of his had talents beyond a kiss.

"Okay, I guess you'll have to settle for old man Tucker."

"You're killing me here."

"You could always give Nate another try. He's a stand-up guy."

"I'm okay with being single." I was okay now, but I wouldn't be okay long term. Maybe I did need to give Nate another look. He was at least in my age range.

We walked out of the diner toward Ana's Jeep as Nate was pulling in to the parking lot. Maybe it was a sign.

"How's the little guy?" Nate rushed over and pulled the blanket from the carrier. "Hey, little man," he said while he rubbed Blue's cheek with one finger.

I watched him go gaga over Blue and thought maybe I'd judged him too quickly. He liked Blue, so who cared if the spark wasn't there between him and me? He'd be a good role model for my son.

"What are you doing this weekend?" The words plopped out of my mouth without much thought. Ana's head snapped in our direction, and a smile spread across her face.

Before Nate could respond, a young, bouncy brunette rushed to his side and kissed him on the cheek. "Sorry I'm late."

Nate looked from Ana to me and announced, "This is Melissa, my girlfriend."

My heart sunk into the pavement. Of course, he had a girlfriend. And of course, she was young and perky with a tight butt and breasts that still sat under her chin.

I plastered on a smile. "Nice to meet you, Melissa."

"Call me Mel," she said in a cheerleader voice that grated on my nerves.

Nate wrapped his arm around the girl's waist and pulled her in close to him. "We're spending the weekend in Denver. Did you need me for something?"

Ana came to the rescue since that's what good friends did. "We're having a barbecue and thought you might like to come."

Mel cocked her head to the side. "A barbecue in the winter?"

I wanted to mimic her by saying, *a barbecue in the winter* in a high-pitched, annoying-as-hell tone, but I didn't. "Unconventional, maybe. Unheard of, no. People eat ribs all year round."

Nate tapped Blue on the nose. "See you soon, buddy." He looked at me and shrugged. "Sorry we have to miss the gathering, but there's a Beyond the Vikings Legend exhibition at the Denver Museum that Mel is dying to see."

"Lord knows you shouldn't pass up a Viking."

"Especially if you're a history major at UC Boulder, like Mel." They started toward the door of the diner. "See you guys later, all right?" Nate said before they walked through the door.

She was cute and peppy and a co-ed. *Just kill me now.* I opened the door and locked the baby's carrier into the car seat frame. I leaned into Blue and whispered, "Looks like Mommy's gonna die alone."

Ana offered to drop me off at the house, but I decided it was time for my Mona fix. She always knew how to cheer me up.

I carried Blue to the door, where Mona greeted us with sass and a smile. "You missed your husband."

"Silas was here?" It was weird but also comforting to refer to him as my husband. I'd been so alone the past few months that even a fake husband was an upgrade. It wasn't the kind of alone that you experienced when no one was around, but the kind of emptiness you felt when people surrounded you and you still felt isolated.

"Come on in." Mona shuffled her sock-covered feet to the side for us to pass. I wondered whether she knew she had put on one pink sock and one red sock. "I still have some hot cocoa."

I was all in when it came to Mona's hot cocoa. In the summer, it was all about the lemonade. In the fall, she transitioned to sweet tea, but at the first snow, it was cocoa all the way. If I wasn't nursing a baby, I could drink the whole batch, but chocolate had caffeine, and caffeine kept Blue up, which kept Mr. Chambers knocking on my door.

I propped the baby seat up on the table and sat across from Mona while we sipped our lukewarm hot chocolate and stared at my little boy. "What do you think of Silas?" I knew Mona didn't know him well because all she ever talked about was Ryker. I was pretty sure she had a cougar crush on the man.

"I like him. I think he'll be good for you."

I set my cup down on the table with a thud. She always gave me the owl cup that had moving eyes, so when I put the cup down, the eyes looked like they were rolling to the ceiling—which was exactly how I felt right then.

"He's not for me. He doesn't even like kids." That wasn't the truth. He didn't say he didn't like kids. He said he couldn't imagine having any of his own. There was a difference, but it was all the same in the end. Kids weren't in his plans.

"I don't think Silas knows what he wants." Mona sloshed the liquid in her cup back and forth. "Those boys have had it rough. No real family, no real roots. You can't want something that you never had. That would be like craving sushi when you've never eaten fish. It won't happen."

Mona's analogies always stumped me, but in a crazy way, they also always made sense. "Regardless, he's a nice guy, and he helped me out of a tricky situation." I explained to Mona about the appearance of my father and how I hadn't been honest about the birth of Blue.

"Why do you think you didn't tell them?" Mona dropped her matchmaker hat and put on her therapist cap. She wore a lot of hats that ranged from comedian to grandmother.

I'd been asking myself that question a lot lately, and what it came down to was, I didn't want my parents' attitude toward children to taint my experience as a mother.

To Mona, I said, "My mother loved me, but she hated me too. I was an unexpected pregnancy like Blue."

"Do you love Blue any less because you didn't plan him? I remember this one time when Troy Higgins and I were at the school planning for the next week. He was a fifth-grade teacher." Mona's light blue eyes lit up at the memory. "He brought in bagels, and I made the coffee."

"What does this have to do with Blue?"

"Nothing, I'm trying to tell you that unexpected things are wonderful."

"Is bagels and coffee a metaphor for sex?"

"No, silly girl, it's bagels and coffee. The sex came later, unexpected, on my desk. I always loved that desk. It's the one I gave you."

I slapped my hands over my eyes. "Gross, I work at that desk."

"I worked at it too. There's nothing wrong with mixing work with pleasure."

I would never be able to sit at that desk and not see Mona sprawled across it.

"Anyway, don't count that boy out. All he needs to see is what a real life looks like." She tipped back her cup and emptied it. When she put the mug down, she had a chocolate mustache. The mother in me grabbed a napkin and cleaned her up.

"I don't know if I'm the one to show him normal. Don't forget, I have an absent mother and a zealot father. I'll be lucky if I can bring Blue up without screwing him up."

"Oh, pish, you're a wonderful mother. Besides, your generation has the Internet, and any question you have can be answered with a click."

"Because it's on the Internet doesn't mean it's true."

"My friend Mabel has been telling me about something called Twatter. What's that?"

I laughed so loud I startled the baby, but he looked straight at Mona and smiled.

"I think you mean Twitter."

"Really? I'm pretty sure she said Twatter. Is it some sex site? That Mabel is worse than me."

I couldn't imagine anyone worse than Mona when it came to the subject of sex. "Maybe she meant Tumblr or Tinder."

"Are those dating sites?"

"Are you looking for a date? If you are, I'd like you to consider Mr. Chambers because maybe if he were getting nookie, he'd leave me alone."

"Chambers is an asshole. Why would I want to date an asshole?"

Why indeed. "I thought you'd consider taking one for the team." I had to rub my eyes to get the vision of Mona and Mr. Chambers doing the dirty out of my mind.

"I'll take one for the team when Tobias Chambers turns into the guy who plays Crixus in *Spartacus*."

I finished my hot cocoa and walked my cup to the sink. "If Mr. Chambers looked like any of the gladiators from *Spartacus*, I'd do him myself." I kissed Mona's cheek and left her to her fantasies.

CHAPTER 9

GRACE

Ana graciously offered to watch Blue while I met my dad for dinner. It wouldn't do any good to bring him. She was right that he fed off my anxiety and fears, and I didn't want him stressed.

I arrived early dressed in black slacks and a white blouse, something I could have never worn if Blue had come with me. Dad didn't put up with tardiness, or much else, for that matter. For a man who had made lots of mistakes in his life, he sure was intolerant of others.

It was one of the reasons I hadn't let him know about Blue. He was supposed to be a religious man who embraced the sinner and not the sin, but Dad was the most judgmental man I knew.

In all honesty, I should have come clean at the start, but no matter how hard I tried, I still wanted to make the man proud. He was my father, after all.

Tripp's Steakhouse wasn't a fancy place, but they did serve a good steak. The host sat me at a table in the center of the room. It was the perfect place to watch people, but it wasn't private by any stretch. Maybe its exposure would keep Dad's outburst in check when I blurted out the truth.

After ordering a club soda, I waited. It didn't take long for him to show up, and by the look on his face, he wasn't too happy. I was about to make his day worse. *It would all be over soon*, I told myself. Sure, he would disown me. I had a kid out of wedlock and lied about it. Whatever he had thought of me yesterday would be so much worse today.

Still scowling, Dad sat in the chair across from me. "Can you believe they have that New Age Bible at the hotel? They're basically heretics."

"You know, Dad, just because people don't believe what you believe doesn't mean they're wrong."

"Sure, it does. There's only one way." He flagged the waitress over and ordered a glass of red wine.

"Your way, right?" I smiled and tried to play it off like I was joking, but I knew I wasn't. It was his way or the highway. I'd chosen the highway a long time ago.

"Where's that man of yours?" Dad looked around the restaurant as if Silas was hiding in a corner.

I took a deep breath and tried to put the right words together in my head. The proper delivery could always smooth the rough edges. "There's something you should know about Silas…"

"He's always late," Silas said, as he walked up to the edge of the table. He was dressed in a pair of khakis and a blue button-down shirt. Dark hair. Blue eyes. Sexy scruff. He pulled preppy off without a hitch. Turns out that Silas was like a chameleon and blended in with whatever. He leaned over and gave me a kiss. It was a sweet, lingering kiss on my lips. "Go with it," he whispered before he stood up. Then he turned toward my dad and shook his hand.

"Nice to see you again, Mr. Faraday." He turned toward me with an expression that said, *let me take care of this*.

"Good to see you, son. You know timeliness is next to godliness."

"Says the man who didn't run into traffic on his way." Silas took a seat to my right and pulled his chair close to mine.

While Dad looked over the menu, I leaned in and whispered, "What are you doing here?"

"You're welcome," he replied and gave me another brush of his lips.

The problem with this ruse was that it felt too good. Sitting here with Silas felt so right, but in a wrong way because there was no truth to it at all. It only prolonged the inevitable: telling Dad that I was a single, unwed mother.

"What brings you to town, sir?"

Dad sat taller when Silas called him sir. "If Grace went to church, she'd know that Father Bradley fell and broke his leg. Since he can't bring Communion to the homebound or visit the sick in the hospital, the deacons in the diocese are filling in. I'm here for a few days to do my part."

Silas nodded his head. "My foster family was Catholic. We went to Mass every Saturday night." I couldn't decide whether that was the truth or whether Silas said that to make my father happy.

Whatever it was, it worked. Dad was smiling for the first time since he'd arrived. "Grace, I'm liking this man more each minute. I might even forgive you for not inviting me to the wedding."

Silas turned to my father and gave him his full attention. "Sir, about the wedding."

I held my breath and waited for him to say that there hadn't been one.

"You not getting invited was my fault. I was desperate for Grace to marry me." He reached up and touched my cheek with such tenderness that I wanted to melt. "Look at her. Who wouldn't want her at home waiting for him?" He dropped his hand and looked back to my dad. "I was going back to a war zone. If I were going to die, I wanted to die a happy, married man."

I saw the tension twitch in his jaw as he recited the lie, but I was sure Dad didn't notice it at all. He was still stuck on the sirs and the mention of weekly Mass.

"I wish you luck with that." My father sipped his wine. His expression was blank, but I knew he had to be thinking about my mom.

Silas raised a brow and reached over to place his hand on mine. "Grace is an amazing woman. She's a wonderful mother." Silas sipped from my club soda since his order hadn't been taken yet. "We didn't tell anyone because we had planned to have a wedding and invite everyone, but then Blue slipped in and things changed."

God, the man was a master with my father. The way he spoke, I almost believed his story. In fact, I closed my eyes and wished that it could have been true. Something about Silas Savage made my heart flutter, and he wasn't even kissing me.

When the waiter came over to take our order, I was grateful for the interruption. Food was always a good conversation starter. Bad or good, I could always talk about food.

Yet I didn't even need it as a fallback topic—the rest of the night went smoothly. Silas talked about his tours in Afghanistan, then I talked about the virtual-assistant company that I'd started six months ago. Of course, Dad talked about the church, but by the end of the night, I could honestly say I'd had a pleasant time and I owed that to Silas.

When Dad left, he gave me a hug—the kind of hug that I'd craved for years. It was the type that said, *I'm proud of you.* He shook hands with Silas and told us he needed to get to the hospital to deliver Communion to the sick, but that he hoped to see him again soon.

As I watched him pull away, guilt poisoned my happy mood. I'd done nothing but extend the deadline to reveal the truth.

"Thank you," I said to the sexy man who stood next to me. "I appreciate you sacrificing time with Ryker to rescue me."

"You're not getting out of it that easy," he said. "I pretended to be your husband and Blue's father, and I didn't even get to sleep with you first. I think you owe me a drink."

I agreed. Though, I probably owed him a lot more than a drink.

He led me to Ryker's car. "We'll leave yours here and pick it up on the way back."

I had no arguments. This was my first time out with a man since I'd become pregnant. Those diner dates with Nate didn't count because I was more interested in the chocolate cake than the man. "Where are we headed?"

Silas opened the door and helped me inside the car before he raced around to climb into the driver's seat. "I wanted to visit this bar called Spurs. It's about twenty minutes outside of town."

Since I hadn't been to many bars in the past year, I was game to visit someplace new, but there were closer places than Spurs. In fact, we could have gone back in the restaurant and had a drink there.

When we pulled up, I was surprised he'd chosen the place. It was straight out of the movie *Easy Rider* with its row of motorcycles out front.

We walked inside and sat at the bar where we both ordered a beer. I'd pumped enough today to get me through the night, so I didn't have to worry about getting Blue tipsy. He didn't mind the bottle as long as it was food.

"Why this place?"

"It's where my parents met," he answered. "I've never seen this place before, actually. I was a kid when they died. Couldn't exactly head to a bar. But I thought about this place a lot. Wanted to see what it looked like."

I felt overwhelmed. I knew the Savage story, and it wasn't pleasant. Three orphaned boys put in an unfair system. One went to jail, the second went in the Army, and the third hasn't yet been found.

I didn't deserve to be here with him in this important moment. Ryker would have been a far better choice than me. "Wouldn't you rather spend this moment with someone else?"

He lifted his hand in the air and waved me off. "Who else is there?"

"Maybe someone you know better than me." The truth was, I knew about Silas's story, but I knew little about the man.

He twisted in his seat and gave me a sly smile. "But sweetheart, we're married."

"Only in our lies." I watched the bubbles float from the bottom of my mug to the top.

"Then let's learn some truths." His leg rubbed against mine and sent a tingle up my spine. "I say we play Never Have I Ever. You know how to play?"

That one was easy. You said *never have I ever* and then finished the sentence with something of your choosing. Anyone who's done that exact thing has to take a drink and loses a point.

"I get to go first." I figured I needed to get the upper hand on this game. "Get your ten fingers up." Silas raised his hands, and so did I. I started out with something I had never done: "Never have I ever run to save my life."

Silas folded in his thumb and took a drink of his beer. "I've run from a lot of things like sniper fire and foster fathers." There was a lot more in that statement that wasn't said. "My turn." He chewed his lower lip and said, "Never have I ever had an STD."

I watched for him to drop a finger, but he didn't. Happily, I couldn't claim that one either. "The only time I ever had unprotected sex was the time I was gifted with boy Blue."

"You've got some shit luck."

"Or maybe it's good luck. His father was an asshole, but he's amazing. My turn." I thought of a dozen things that I wanted to know, but I could only choose one. "Never have I ever had a one-night stand." I lowered my finger and reached for my beer. Silas did the same. We were equally matched with our moral fiber.

We went back and forth asking mostly sexual questions like "Never have I ever had sex with more than one person at the same time" and "Never have I ever paid someone for sex or been paid for sex." Neither of us lost a point with those. I said, "Never have I ever cheated on someone I dated," and that was a no for both of us. It was nice to know that Silas was faithful if he was committed.

He said, "Never have I ever been the other woman or man," and raised an eyebrow curiously when I folded a finger down. I had to be honest. While I hadn't known that Trenton Kehoe was married at the time, the fact was, I'd still slept with him.

After I explained my story, Silas shook his head sympathetically. "What an ass," he said.

"Never have I ever been a victim of a crime." I don't know why I said it but the minute the words came out Silas's face turned white. "I'm sorry, you don't have to answer that."

He took a long drink of his beer, gulping until it was empty. After asking the bartender for a refill, he spoke again. "Ryker killed our foster father for me. He went to jail for six years."

As he was picking up his fresh beer, my phone rang. It was Ana, and it wasn't good.

"Grace, you need to come to the hospital. Blue is sick."

CHAPTER 10

SILAS

I knew something was wrong as soon as Grace answered the phone. Her face turned pale, and a look of fear flashed in her eyes.

"We'll be there as soon as we can." Grace picked up her purse and started running toward the door. "Blue's at the hospital."

I tossed a twenty on the bar and chased after her. She was yanking on the driver's door when I made it outside, and tears had started to fall.

"I've got the keys, I'm driving." I opened the passenger door and gestured for her to get in. "I didn't drink that much. I only had a beer and a half, which is weird, because I'm usually the crazy one in any crowd." I made sure she was buckled in before racing to the driver's side.

"Are you sure you can drive?"

"Grace, I drink regularly, which means that beer won't affect me as much. When's the last time you had a drink?"

She knew I was right. She was tipsy after the first half beer. Alcohol had a way of sneaking up on you when you hadn't had it in a while.

I started the engine and turned onto the highway toward Boulder.

"Oh, my God, drive faster. Ana said he had a rash. What if it's measles or mumps or rubella?"

"Is he vaccinated?"

She looked at me like I was out of my mind. "He's only a month old, of course not."

I pressed the gas pedal farther down and sped up to five over the limit.

"What are his symptoms?" I wasn't in the medical field, but I'd roomed with a medic for a long time. "Maybe it's an allergy."

Grace snapped at me. "What the hell do you know anyway? You don't even like babies."

That hurt—I *did* like babies. Long ago, I'd even dreamed of having a family someday. But then I saw what family looked like in foster care and decided to take a pass.

I let the comment slide, though, since she was clearly emotional, and for good reason. "Call Ana back and ask what they think it is," I said instead.

Grace tried to call back, but we were in a dead zone between the peaks. Her silent tears turned into straight-out-uncontrollable sobs.

When we got to the hospital, I'd barely stopped the car before she jumped out and ran into the emergency room entrance.

I parked the car and started toward the hospital. Ryker met me in the parking lot. "Blue is going to be okay. They think it's a milk protein allergy."

"Thank God. I swear Grace nearly ripped my head off while I was trying to get her here."

"Man, you can't get between a lioness and her cub." He patted me on the back and walked with me into the hospital. I hated the smell of antiseptic. It reminded me of death and lost dreams.

"Was Mom ever that protective?"

Ryker's eyes widened. "You don't remember that time when Dan Clover was picking on you in kindergarten?"

"Hell, yeah. That bastard used to steal my snack every day." I thought back to the day when Mom told me to let him have it. I hadn't understood why she'd wanted me to give over my cheese and crackers so easily. "Oh, right. She put cayenne pepper in the cheese one time. I remember him crying because his mouth burned so much." *Yep, our mom was a lioness.*

"Never question the fact that Mom and Dad loved us. They gave us everything they could."

"Oh, please—" I leaned against the brick wall of the building.

Ryker stood before me and held up his hand to stop me mid-sentence.

"I rarely pull out the big brother card, but I have to now. Now that I'm going to be a dad, I've given a lot of thought to what I want to do with my life. My choices affect Ana and our baby." He moved to my side and leaned against the wall next to me.

"You're not planning to run a motorcycle gang, are you?" I said sarcastically.

He scrubbed his hands through his hair. "Rooster, listen to me." He only used my nickname when he was serious. "How many of your soldier friends have kids?"

"Tons. What's your point?"

"I imagine when one of them dies in war, not all the family are saying things like 'He died for his country,' or 'He died doing what he loved.' There's always going to be the one who says, 'Why would he stay in the Army when he had kids? He knew the risk.'"

"The same could be said about police officers and firefighters. Jobs where you put your life on the line each day. What about the guy who climbs telephone poles, or the electrician who deals with massive voltage each day?"

"Not the same. They don't bring their kids to the front lines." I knew I had him there, but Ryker had a point to make.

"Dad's career choice wasn't gang leader. He was a motorcycle mechanic who happened to call a bunch of bikers, family."

"I'm not going to argue with you, but what family packs the kind of munitions it took to take down everyone in that building? I almost lost you too, or did you forget that you laid in the hospital for a week in intensive care?"

"I'll never forget that day." He set his hand on my shoulder. "It was the worst day of my life, but it taught me an invaluable lesson. Actually, you taught me an invaluable lesson, which has been solidified by Ana's love."

"Oh, do tell."

"Family comes first. Remember when I wondered if Decker wouldn't be better off without us? I was wrong."

I pushed off the wall and forced Ryker's hand to drop from my shoulder. "Before you go on, I wanted to talk to you about that. Maybe you were right." I looked toward the sliding doors and wished I'd gone inside instead of staying outside talking. "Maybe Decker would be better off living oblivious to the facts of his life." I turned and walked toward the door.

Ryker's boots pounded out a heavy rhythm behind me. "You're wrong. Family is everything."

"Come on, Hawk. Chances are he lives in the 'burbs with his accountant father and his schoolteacher mother. Besides, it's a moot point. Didn't you tell me that the PI came to a dead end on the last lead?"

"He's family. Are you telling me you believe he'd be better off without us? What happened to the guy who said, 'Sell everything, we have to find our brother'? What the hell happened to that guy? I want my brother, Silas, back. When you find him, tell him I'd love to talk to him."

CHAPTER 11

GRACE

Ana was in the waiting room when I arrived. She looked worn out and tired and pale. She twisted and turned the hem of her shirt until it wrapped around her hand. Her eyes lifted.

"Oh, my God, you're here." She dropped the wrinkled hem and rushed toward me, throwing her arms around my neck. "They took him back for testing." She dragged me to the intake window. "This is Blue's mother," she told the nurse sitting behind the glass.

The woman pushed a button, and the door next to us swung open. "Come on back."

"Wouldn't they let you go in with him?" We rushed through the door and followed the woman to a nearby curtain where there was an empty bed and bassinet.

"Yes, but then they took him, and I thought I'd wait for you."

"What happened?"

A tear slipped from Ana's eye. "I don't know, I fed him, and he fell asleep in my arms, and then minutes later he got all splotchy, and he sounded like he was having a tough time breathing, so I called you while Ryker rushed us here. They think it's an allergic reaction."

I collapsed on the bed with guilt eating at my insides. Poor Blue was suffering because I'd eaten something he couldn't handle. "It was probably the damn enchiladas and beans and salsa."

"Who knows? Babies are sensitive. Don't beat yourself up." She sat on the bed next to me and pulled me in for a hug. "You're an amazing mom."

"I'm making it up as I go."

The nurse peeked in from behind the curtain and said, "There are two men in the waiting room pacing back and forth. I can't let them back here because there's a two-person limit."

"I'll go," Ana said immediately.

"Blue is seeing the pediatric allergy specialist," the nurse said. "It will be a while." She waved at us to follow her. "I can get you both when they bring him back down. He'll be fine. A little epinephrine made him right as rain."

I looked at Ana. "We'll both go. It doesn't do any good for me to be sitting here by myself. Besides, I have to thank Silas for getting me here so fast. I think I yelled at him, and it wasn't his fault."

Ana and I walked to the door and waited for the nurse to push the button for it to open. "He's a Savage, he can handle it." Her voice confident and unwavering. So unlike the girl who had twisted her shirt only minutes ago.

I headed straight for Silas while Ana went for Ryker. Both men greeted us with open arms. I rested my head against Silas's chest and breathed in his calming scent. He wore some kind of cologne that smelled like citrus and sex appeal.

"I'm sorry for yelling at you." I looked up into his big blue expressive eyes and nearly melted. He barely even knew me, and yet I could see his concern.

"Never apologize for acting like a good mom." He kissed the top of my head in such a familiar way it almost felt like we were truly a couple.

"Grace?" a familiar voice called out.

Could this day get any worse? I turned away from Silas to see my dad standing behind me. "What are you doing here?" I asked, then remembered him telling us he was bringing Communion to the sick.

"I told you I had people to see." He stepped closer and stared at me. "Why are you here? I left you hours ago. You should have been home."

"Silas and I stayed out a bit longer." I took a deep breath and swallowed hard. "Blue reacted to something in the milk when Ana was feeding him."

My father leaned in and smelled my breath. In that moment, I was back in high school. I'd never made it into the house without a full sobriety check. Funny thing was, I never drank. I was a high-on-life girl. Being out with friends was all I needed to feel good.

"You've been drinking." His voice was clipped and accusatory. "What kind of mother are you?"

I took a step back and found myself pressed against Silas's body. He was a sturdy wall behind me. "I'm a good parent, which is more than I can say for you."

My dad reared back and raised his hand as though he would hit me until Silas stepped to the side and grabbed his arm. There was a fire in his eyes that made me half afraid of him. It titillated the other half of me.

"I'd think twice about raising your hand to my wife, Deacon Faraday. You lay a hand on her and you'll be calling for a priest to recite your *last* rites." He emphasized the word *last* to make a point. "You ask Grace what kind of mother she is, and yet you're a despicable father. A loving father would never hurt his child, no matter what." Silas let go of my dad's arm with a push.

"I'm worried about my grandson. He deserves better than Grace." Dad rubbed at the place on his wrist where Silas had gripped him.

Silas stepped forward in a menacing fashion, and my father stumbled back. My heart raced … not out of fear or anger, but exhilaration. It was about time Dad found someone he couldn't torment. "She deserved better than you. A man like you raised me. You know what happened to him?"

Dad took a step back. "I have no idea." The look in his eyes said he didn't want to know.

"He picked on the wrong boy and died."

My dad's face turned pale. "You killed him?"

Silas shook his head. "Let's say karma has a way of coming back and kicking you in the ass." Silas wrapped his arm around my dad's shoulders and walked him to the door. "It's time for you to leave. No one needs your brand of help here." He gave my dad a shove out the door and walked back with his hands in his pockets and his head hung low.

"Thank you, Silas. You always seem to save me." I watched the man in front of me. He was simple and sexy and had his own scars inside. Who would save Silas?

"I apologize for stepping into your family matter. It's just …" He rubbed his scruffy chin between his thumb and fingers. "I won't stand back and watch a man hit a woman."

This was the first time a man had ever stuck up for me. The first time one had come to my rescue. The first time I felt like my value wasn't found solely between my legs.

I lifted on my tiptoes and kissed him like my life depended on it. I hoped he felt my gratefulness in the gesture.

A soft male voice came from behind me. "Ms. Faraday?"

I swung around to face a man in a white jacket with the name Dr. Templeton embroidered on the pocket.

"Yes?"

He introduced himself as a pediatric allergist and explained that it looked like Blue had a milk protein allergy. He also said maternal stress during pregnancy increased allergy susceptibility and asked if I had experienced undue stress during Blue's gestation.

I let out a laugh. "If you count having an asshole as your baby's father, making a major move, undergoing a career change, and being a single mother as stressful, then yes."

The doctor looked behind me at Silas and frowned. There was an awkward silence, and I knew he thought I had referred to him as the asshole father.

"He's not Blue's father."

The doctor smiled, nodded diplomatically, and then changed the subject. He handed me a list of milk-protein-free formulas. "I know you're nursing your son, and generally we'd recommend that, but since Blue had such a serious reaction, I'd recommend formula for him unless you want to switch your diet. And given that he had such a severe reaction, I wouldn't recommend it."

I looked down at the list. I'd breastfed Blue for several reasons. One, it was supposed to be healthier for him. Two, it was cost-effective.

"You're sure these won't bother him?"

"We tried this one in the nursery." He pointed to the brand that said Enfamil. "He did fine with it. Are you ready to take your son home?"

"Yes." I said with the enthusiasm of a girl being asked to prom.

Fifteen minutes later, Blue was buckled into his car seat, and Ana and I were on our way to my house.

Silas and Ryker took off together and mentioned something about stopping at the bar for a beer and a game of pool.

CHAPTER 12

SILAS

The next morning, I stood outside The Nest with Ryker by my side. Although I'd been in the house once since my return, I hadn't set foot in the garage. What I expected to find when I walked inside, I wasn't sure.

"You ready?" Ryker held the handle to the garage door and pulled it up. This wasn't part of the original building. It used to have a solid garage door that tilted up. This was an upgrade.

I held my breath as the metal wheels rolled inside the channel and the door opened to reveal a floor covered in tools, not the blood and bodies I saw inside my head.

Never seeing it again after the shootings had probably been worse for my six-year-old imagination. When I closed my eyes, I had visions of spraying blood and body parts, not a garage floor stained by oil and littered with wrenches and sockets.

"I like what you've done with the place."

Ryker walked inside and picked up the tools that lay around a Harley he'd been working on. "I think I leave shit lying around to see if Dad's spirit will come down and slap me upside the head."

"Do you remember his belt?" The damn belt had a buckle the size of Texas. Ryker had gotten it once across his ass for fibbing, and from that point on, all it took was the mention of the belt to straighten us up. Being the younger brother had its advantages. You got to see what the older sibling got an ass beating for, and either you didn't do it, or you did it smarter. Decker never had to experience the fear of Raptor Savage.

"Remember? Hell, I can still feel his belt." Ryker moved his hand to his ass and rubbed it like he was feeling the sting then.

I thought back to the hospital last night when Grace's father had raised his hand in anger. There were few times when a swat did a child good. Times like when they ran into the street and nearly got run over. Or maybe when they stole all the money from their mama's wallet and bought ten boxes of Red Hots, then ate them all at one sitting. Maybe not then because the stomachache was punishment enough. But definitely not when they hired a responsible babysitter so they could go out for dinner and a drink, just to have a break. And a closed-or open-handed hit was never acceptable.

I shifted my thoughts from Dad's belt to Dad's workshop. While Ryker tossed tools into the chest, I walked around the space. I could see it like it was twenty years ago. There were motorcycles waiting in line for Dad's magic hands. People would wait for weeks because he was that good.

I brushed my fingers along a wooden post and let the tips run into the divots I imagined had been caused by bullets. My eyes skimmed the floor looking for clues, but there were none. It was a garage, and the ghosts of my past I expected to see didn't exist.

"So, I thought that if you came back, we could run the garage together. You're organized and good with numbers. I'm good with bikes or anything with a small engine. Now that Sam Junior and I aren't at odds anymore, business has been picking up."

I leaned against the wood post and crossed my arms. Ryker wasn't listening. I had every intention of going back to the desert. Over there, all I had to do was be a soldier and survive. Here, so much more was expected of me.

"I'm not staying. As soon as I get that call, I'm out of here." I kicked off the post and walked to the empty office. "Besides," I said with a hint of humor in my voice, "how am I supposed to keep the books when you gave the office furniture away?"

Ryker slammed the lid to the tool chest closed and stalked toward me. He was always bigger than me until I joined the Army. I worked out every day and built muscle on muscle to make sure that no one could ever do to me again what that asshole had done.

I had come a long way from that day. Ryker thought I stayed in the desert because I craved the adrenaline rush. There was truth to that, but the deepest, brutal truth was that sticking close to my family made me vulnerable to horrific things.

Ryker walked past me and slid down the wall to sit on the cement floor. "Do you blame me for what Troy did to you?"

I wasn't expecting that question. It was a hard one to answer, so I dodged it. "Do you blame me for the six years you spent in jail?" I watched him and didn't see a flinch or flicker in his expression.

"No, I blame myself for everything."

I chuckled at the insanity of our lives. "I blame myself for the time you served. If I had stayed with my other foster families, our lives would have been different." I folded my legs and sat on the cold concrete floor.

"You understood the importance of family. You knew we were all we had, and to let that go meant to give up. You never gave up."

"They say hindsight is twenty-twenty. If I had stayed in one of those homes, I wouldn't have been a pawn in Troy's game. He wouldn't have used me to get to you. You wouldn't have gone to prison. I wouldn't have … well, you know."

"I'm sorry." Ryker let his head fall forward.

There were two days in my life that changed everything. The first was when our parents died on the cold cement floor of this garage. The second was the day Ryker killed the man who abused me. Both days had made me into who I was, and I wasn't sure whether that was bad or good.

I looked at my brother, who was still beating himself up over the past. "You have nothing to be sorry about. Troy beat me all the time, but he beat all of us. And that thing you're thinking about … it happened once, and you made sure it would never happen again. That makes you my hero."

"Is this where we are supposed to shed a tear and hug?" Ryker struggled to stand, and when he did, he offered me a hand up.

As soon as I was on my feet and out of his reach, I said, "Piss off."

"I won't stop trying to get you to stay."

I followed him into the main garage and up the stairs to the house above. We had started the repairs the day I met Grace, but there was a long way to go. Time hadn't been kind to the old house. "I won't stay." I closed the door behind us. "Once this place is fixed up, you should sell it."

"What about Decker? This belongs to him too."

"Then when you sell it, use my portion to find him so you can give him his share."

I didn't want to get into the Decker conversation again. All my life, I'd wanted to find him, but lately, I'd been thinking about what would happen if we did. Would he want to know his parents were killed on their property? That one brother murdered a man to protect the other? That I was so screwed up I couldn't stay in one place because allowing anyone to get close was too risky? I was certain that Decker was better off not knowing us.

"You can be such an ass." He turned and walked to the door. "I'm going home. Do what you want up here alone because, Silas, the one thing I've learned from you and Ana is that family is everything, and being alone is overrated."

He trotted down the steps, and I listened for the garage door to close. Once it did, I walked back to the room Ryker and I used to share. I hadn't been in it since that day, and walking into the blue room now was like getting hit over the head with a hammer.

Outside of getting rid of the furniture and clothes, he had done little with it. My scribbled-on art remained stuck to the door with yellowed tape. Magazine cutouts of Harley Davidson motorcycles decorated the walls. Even the black ink stain from when I broke a pen was still on the hardwood floor. It was funny how some things changed while others stayed the same.

As I reached for the worn-out art, my phone rang. Thinking it was Ryker, I pulled it from my pocket and let my finger hover over the ignore button. But it wasn't him; it was First Sergeant Taylor.

My gut knotted up the same way it did before a raid. Endorphins were pumping, and a sick feeling washed over me. On the third ring, I answered.

"Sergeant Savage speaking." I stood up straight and tall, the way I would if I were standing before the man himself. I had a lot of respect for my sergeant. He'd never steered me wrong, and he always went to bat for me. "What news do you have for me?"

Too many tours in the desert had taken their toll on my lungs. Occupational lung disease was what they called it. Smoke from the burn pits, aerosolized metals from exploded IEDs and ordinance, and dust from the sand had worked their way into my lung tissue.

I placed my hand over my chest and breathed deep. I felt fine—most of the time. A little winded when I exerted myself too much, but it wasn't like I had to run ten miles a day with a rucksack. Most of the time we drove or walked.

"I spoke to the medical board. It's a no, son." His voice lowered to whisper levels. "I'm afraid you're out."

"But I'm all healed up," I said. "My lungs feel fine."

"I understand that," the sergeant said. "But my hands are tied. Uncle Sam has decided. Take the retirement, son. You've earned it."

"Take it and do what?" I screamed into the phone. "The Army is what I am. It's what I do."

"Not anymore, Silas." It was the first time he'd ever called me by my first name, and I knew it was because he no longer considered me a comrade.

I hung up the phone and punched a hole in the wall. I wanted my life to stay the same, but I was in for a big freaking change.

CHAPTER 13

GRACE

Blue sucked down the foul-smelling formula the hospital had given me last night. If it smelled this bad going in, what would it be like coming out?

I pulled the bottle from his lips. He didn't love the rubber nipple, but he loved to eat, so he figured it out. What was it about men and nipples?

Looking down, I saw he was doing much better. His skin was pink and soft, and the blotchy patches had all but disappeared.

"Hey, buddy." I used the name Silas had given Blue the night I met him. "I'm so sorry. Mommy didn't mean to make you sick with what she ate." I couldn't shake the guilt that sat heavy on my chest. I didn't do it on purpose, but it reinforced the point that every decision I made affected my son.

His eyes drooped closed, and the nipple fell from his lips. I wiped the dribble of creamy formula from his mouth and lifted him to my shoulder. Once I got one good burp out of him, I walked him back to his room and put him in his crib. I turned up the baby monitor and tiptoed back to the living room.

Now that Blue wasn't eating what I did, I had free rein to drink real coffee. Five minutes later, I sat on the couch sipping a cup of the best coffee I'd had in at least nine months. With the press of a finger, American Movie Classics flashed to life on the television as a knock sounded on the door.

I never had a minute of peace to myself. I supposed I would have to get used to that.

When I opened the door, my father stood there. He lowered his head like a penitent seeking forgiveness. "Can we talk?"

I opened the door wide and let him enter. He looked around my house like he was taking inventory.

"Coffee?" I asked.

He nodded, and I pointed to the sofa. Dad liked his coffee black. In his life, everything was black and white—or at least he thought it was. But in real life, there were many shades of gray.

He took the cup I offered and sat in the red chair.

"I'm sorry about last night."

My hand jerked in surprise, and I almost spilled my coffee. My father never apologized. It was one reason Mom lived a separate life from him. He'd told her that his sins were between the good Lord and him, and he didn't owe her anything but his last name. When my father had given up his mistress, he'd married the church instead. Whether it was the mistress or the church, they were both demanding lovers.

I remembered the Bible verse about doing unto others and thought, *oh, what the hell.* "I accept your apology." I sipped my coffee and stared at the man who sat in my house. I barely knew him. And the sad part was how I had no desire to develop a relationship with him.

The problem with having him around was that he could be an influence in Blue's life, and I didn't want my son growing up to be anything like his grandfather.

Dad was apologizing for last night, but what about the thousands of other transgressions and hurtful words he had hurled at me over the past twenty-six years?

"I overreacted."

I wanted to roll my eyes and scream, "understatement," but I didn't because it would serve no purpose.

Dad scooted forward and set his half-empty cup on my recently delivered coffee table. "Blue is my first grandchild, and I want to be part of this new family's life." He craned his neck to look past me and down the hallway. "Where's that husband of yours? I'm pretty sure he owes me an apology too."

I didn't know what twisted my gut more. Was it that my dad had asked for my fake husband, and I would have to come clean right now? Or was it because he considered Silas's protection of me an act that required an apology?

"Silas isn't here."

He looked at his watch. "It's eight o'clock, where in the heck is he?"

I sat up straight and steeled myself for his wrath. "Dad, Silas doesn't live here."

He narrowed his eyes at me. "Just like your mother, aren't you?"

I knew what he meant. He was referring to the fact that he and my mother hadn't been a real married couple for decades. It was in name only. "No, Silas never lived here. He's not who you think he is."

"What ... are you telling me you're not married to that man? That he knocked you up and won't take responsibility?" Dad rose from his seat and paced the room. "I'll get him to step up."

Like you did? What Dad didn't understand was his presence didn't count as actual parental participation. "He didn't knock me up. Blue isn't Silas's son." There was an ache in my throat that felt like I'd swallowed glass.

"You lied?" he yelled.

"Dad, the baby is sleeping," I whispered, trying to keep the situation from turning nuclear.

"You lied, Grace."

"Yes, but you have to ask yourself why. Look at what you're doing. You're judging me and bullying me."

"I'm not judging you. I call it like I see it. You're a damn slut, Grace. Now tell me who Blue's father is."

He towered over me, and in an instant, I turned into a little girl in trouble. "He's not in the picture."

"What's his name, Grace? I'm not leaving without a name." He plopped back into the red chair and disrespected my space by kicking his feet up on my new table. The table Ryker made solid with wood glue and screws. "Is he married?"

Leave it to Dad to latch on to the only shame I felt regarding Blue's conception. How could he know? Did he have some superpower? Was it because he was a cheater he recognized something in me? I hadn't knowingly helped a man cheat. I buried my head in my hands. "I didn't know."

"You're a damn home-wrecker?"

Anger boiled inside me. "Like you have room to talk. You allowed another woman inside your marriage, and it ruined all of our lives. Why did you stay with Mom if you two are so unhappy?"

Dad gave me a deadpan look like the answer was obvious. "We're Catholic."

I looked up at him like he spoke in tongues. "Step into the twenty-first century. People get divorced. Women don't need men to have babies, and not every woman who sleeps with more than one man is a slut."

He rolled forward and stood to hover above me like a dark cloud. "Give me a name, Grace." His voice was serial-killer cold.

I didn't want to give him anything, but Dad was like a dog with a bone. He wasn't going anywhere until he knew. "Trenton Kehoe, and he asked me to abort Blue."

Dad stalked toward the front door and flung it open. "You're a total disappointment. You should have given that baby to someone who would raise it right. I'm done with you." He slammed the door after he walked out, which woke Blue. By the time I got to his crib, we were both crying.

I got him changed and dressed and walked him down to the place where no one called me a slut. Where no one made me feel less than what I was. Where people loved me no matter what. I walked him down to Mona's because she—not that horrible man who'd walked out on me—was family.

"Come on in," she said the minute the door opened. "Give me that boy, and you go make us some coffee." She held out her arms, and when I put my whimpering son into them, she took him to a big black leather chair I hadn't seen before. "Ana says he's off the teat, so make it real and make it strong."

I dumped the grounds into the percolator. I swear it was the same model that Ana's grams had owned, only this one worked.

When I came back into the living room, Blue was cooing and looking up at Mona like he was in love. She softly sang him a song that went something like this: *Good morning, good morning, we'll dance the whole day through, good morning, good morning to you.*

I looked at the clock on the wall. "It's not morning, it's nearly noon."

Mona huffed. "He doesn't know." She kicked out the footrest on her chair and reclined with Blue on her chest. He kind of looked perfect there, and for the first time in a long time, I was glad I moved to Fury. Here he had a family. He had an aunt and an uncle, and he had Mona, who was the best grandma a baby could ever ask for.

"My dad disowned me today. It all came out about Silas not being my husband or Blue's father."

Mona made a tsk sound, which meant I was in for a few words of wisdom. "Someone once told me that the truth costs nothing, but a lie can cost everything."

The air took on the comforting scent of fresh-brewed coffee, and I relaxed back on the overstuffed sofa. It was a place I'd spent many a day watching *Judge Judy* with Mona while my body worked hard to create my perfect son.

"I didn't set out to lie."

She shifted Blue around and cradled him in her arms. For a woman who had never given birth to children, she was such a nurturer, but then again, she'd had children—hundreds of them if you count thirty years as an elementary-school teacher.

"Lies come in many forms. Go get our coffee and we'll talk about it."

I rushed into the kitchen and poured us both a cup. When I returned, she was cooing and smiling at Blue. He had that effect on everyone. Blue was like a bridge of goodness between everyone but my father and me. "Teach me something."

That was Mona's specialty. It didn't matter whether she was talking about men's parts or the price of petroleum; there was always a lesson to be learned.

"We all lie, whether it's to ourselves or to others. Take me, for example. I pretend I'm not going blind, but I am. You pretend that running your business and taking care of Blue will be enough, but it won't. Ryker told himself that he was a bad person, but he isn't. Ana, well … I'm not sure that girl has ever lied on purpose. Silas is lying to himself if he thinks he can be an island. We all lie, but it's understanding why we lie that's important."

"I can't answer that question."

"I can answer it for you. Your mom and dad have never been there, and that's been hard on you. I would imagine you didn't tell them about Blue because you don't want them to disapprove of him. And I think there's a piece of you that wishes things were different—a piece of you wishes you were enough. Telling your dad everything he wanted to hear was probably like asking him to like you."

Mona was right. She was always right. "There's no pleasing my father." Conflicting emotions tore me apart. Pride and disappointment. Concern and indifference. Love and hate.

"That's my point. You can't be responsible for his happiness, but he should have been responsible for yours."

"How so?"

"You didn't ask to be born. Your parents brought you into this world, and they had a responsibility to give you the best life they could. Did they?"

I sipped my coffee and thought about her statement. "No." My whole life, I proved them right or proved them wrong. There was no middle ground, but I never gave up trying to please them, and I never thought about their responsibility to please me.

We sat in silence for a while. "How did you get so philosophical?"

"You don't get to be in your seventies and not learn a thing or two."

I stared at the chair that seemed to swallow her up. "Why the new chair?"

She took her free hand and rubbed the soft leather armrest like she was caressing a lover's thigh. "Mabel and I went to Denver to that American Furniture Warehouse. All I had to do was sit in it once."

"That good, huh?"

Mona laughed. "You know what they say. Once you go black, you never go back."

I busted a big belly laugh. "I'm not sure they were talking about chairs." I set my coffee on the table and took in the woman who brightened my dullest day. I'd be lying to myself if I said she wasn't one of the best things to ever happen to me.

CHAPTER 14

SILAS

"Do you want to tell me why there is a hole in our bedroom wall upstairs?" Ryker didn't sound upset. He sounded concerned. Punching walls was his thing, not mine, and looking down at my swollen knuckles, I now understood why I never adopted self-mutilation or home demolition as a coping mechanism. Nope, I stuck myself in the middle of a war zone and figured if I made it out, then that was the way it was supposed to be. I took the fatalistic attitude.

"Got some bad news for me and some good news for you." I leaned against the bike he was working on. "Looks like I'm staying."

Ryker jumped up and pulled me into his arms. "That's great." It was funny how one man's joy could become another's misery. "What changed your mind?"

"Nothing changed my mind. The Army changed its mind. Seems I have a lung problem that won't get better if I stay in the desert, and I'm not becoming a desk jockey, so I'm out." I couldn't believe how painful admitting that felt. I'd been burned and stabbed and beaten to within an inch of my life and shrugged it off, but letting go of the Army eviscerated me.

Ryker stepped back and looked at me. "I'm so sorry." His words held remorse, but his face held the expression of a man overjoyed.

This garage. This town. It had taken the lives of my parents, and I felt like it was coming after me next.

"Can I borrow your car? I need to clear my head, and I think a drive would do me good."

"I can do better than my old Subaru. It's a nice day. I've got a bike here that needs a test drive. You want to take it for a spin?"

I looked down at the cherry red Harley and nodded. The wind in my hair and the town at my back sounded pretty damn good.

Ryker handed me the key and stood back. "Now that you're staying, do you want to keep looking for Decker?" He walked to a wall where he pulled an older photo from a tack. Sitting under the old oak tree out front were Ryker, Ana, and me holding Decker. It was taken on Easter Sunday before everything went to shit.

I stared at the picture and wondered if we could have it all again. I wasn't sure. Hell, I wasn't sure about anything anymore, but it wasn't fair to Ryker to give up. "Have the detective keep looking," I said and handed him the photo, "but I don't want to know about it unless he comes back with something solid." I climbed on the bike and started it. Over the idling engine, I yelled, "I can't take any more disappointment!"

A twist of the throttle made the bike growl. It had been a long time since I had a motorcycle beneath me. There weren't a lot of Harley-Davidson bikes sitting around in Kandahar Province.

I shifted it into gear and took off. The road rushed beneath me. The wind beat against my face and body. I leaned back and let the bike take me where it wanted.

Just as I was getting a feel for it and the road, I saw the flashing lights behind me. I pulled over and waited for the officer to approach.

"You got a license for that bike?" The officer walked toward me, and once he was in front of me, he widened his eyes. "Silas?"

I looked at his nametag. "Sheriff Stuart. Junior?"

"The same, except I don't go by Junior. Makes me feel like a kid." He walked around the bike. "Yours?"

"Nope, and I don't have a motorcycle license. I was taking it out on a test drive." I pulled my license and military ID out of my wallet.

He took them from my hand, and after giving them a cursory look, he handed them back. "You back for a while?"

I looked past the man who had spent years terrorizing my brother and wondered how we'd gotten to this place. "I'm back for a bit. You gonna write me a ticket or what?"

The sheriff chuckled. "You want a ticket?"

I shrugged. "Not particularly, but you got to do what you got to do."

"If you stay, you should apply for a job at the sheriff's department."

Now it was my turn to laugh. "Can you imagine the town of Fury with an officer named Savage?"

The sheriff adjusted his hat. "Stranger things have happened. Look at your brother and me. Who would have thought we'd become friends?" He turned and walked to his car. Before he climbed in, he called over, "Take it easy on that bike."

The sheriff made a U-turn and headed back to Fury. I climbed back on the bike and drove the opposite direction.

Fifteen miles out of town, I came upon a broken-down car with a blonde waving her hands in the air. I whipped the bike around and went to help. I had no idea what I would do with the rest of my life, but I knew what I'd be doing for the next few minutes and that was a start.

I might have been an asshole to some, but when it came to women and children, I was a downright knight in shining armor. Maybe it was because I'd seen so much abuse in my life, or maybe it was because by the time I was six years old, my mother had already taught me to be the right kind of man when it came to the fairer sex. I had limited memories, but I remember my mother telling me to treat a woman like she was a prize.

As I neared at a slower speed, I recognized the girl as the waitress from the diner. I parked the bike next to her blue Honda Civic and climbed off.

"Hannah, right?"

"That's me, and you're Silas."

"You got it." I looked at the opened hood on her car. "What's going on?"

In blue jeans, a pink fuzzy sweater, and boots, Hannah wasn't dressed for work. She looked more like she was heading out on a date. Her hair was down, her makeup on, but that chip she seemed to carry on her shoulder was still in place.

"Well," she began, "since your brother isn't single anymore, I have to branch out. I have a lunch date with a guy in Pine Creek." She tossed her hair over her shoulder and looked at her car. "I was driving along and hit a giant pothole. There was this big bang, and I pulled over to see what it was. Once I turned off my car, I couldn't get it started again. Can you help?"

I wasn't the mechanic in the family—that was Ryker—but I looked under the hood for something obvious. When I saw the battery cable off the terminal, I knew why her car wouldn't start.

"Have you met this guy before, or is it a blind date?" It wasn't any of my business, but I spent eight years hanging out with men, and they could be total jerks. Despite Hannah's obsession with my brother, she seemed like a nice girl, and I didn't want to see her get used.

"Blind date, but I'm sure it will be fine. He's the mayor's son." She gave me a smug look. "There aren't many single men under fifty in town. I got excited to meet you, but you're not single either."

I tightened down the cable and shut the hood. "Of course, I am." I smiled at her.

"Yeah. Sure, you are." She climbed inside her car, and it started right away.

"Be safe on your date," I called as she pulled away. I looked at the tail end of her car as it disappeared up the road and wondered what the hell she'd meant by that.

I climbed back on the Harley and took off, but Hannah's words played in my head, and Grace's face was the one I saw each time I blinked. Could I ever be what she needed? I considered Blue, and my heart raced. Being with Grace excited me. Being something to Blue terrified me. To open my heart would mean risking it. Hadn't I lost enough?

A few minutes later, I found myself stopping in a park next to a white SUV. I looked out to find the sexy redhead I'd been thinking about sitting on a blanket in front of the lake. Her head moved back and forth as if she was in deep conversation, but the only one around was Blue, and he didn't seem to answer back.

CHAPTER 15

GRACE

Shattered was the best word to describe how I felt. I'd always been disconnected from my family, but I'd never been disowned.

"What father does such a thing?" I looked down at my boy and realized that he and I were a lot alike. My father disowned me when he realized I wouldn't be his picture of a perfect daughter. Trenton Kehoe never gave his son a chance.

"I don't know what's worse, knowing your father and having him toss you aside or knowing he never cared about you to begin with."

It was crazy to sit on a blanket at a park and discuss the injustices of life with an infant, but somehow it gave me strength.

I looked down at my phone to see if Dad had returned any of my calls. I'd left at least three messages asking him what *I'm done with you* meant. His silence was my answer. He

was done.

"I'll never abandon you, Blue. I will be here for you every step of the way. I don't care if you bring home an A or F. I won't care if you screw the entire cheerleading squad as long as you treat them right. All I care about is you."

He lay on his back and kicked out his legs and arms. I laid my hand on his chest where his heart beat under my palm.

"Know that you will always be the most important thing in my life … no matter what."

"That's a nice speech," a voice said from above me. I looked up and saw Silas, and my heart danced with excitement. "I like the part about the cheerleading squad." He pulled out his phone and pointed it at me. "Mind if I record that so when it happens, he has proof that you won't hang him by his nut sack?"

I ran my fingers through my hair and held my hand up to block my face. "You don't need to record that, I'm a woman of my word."

Silas nodded and looked at the blanket before him. "Can I join you?"

I moved over and made room for him next to me, but he moved to the other side of Blue. "How long have you been listening?" I swallowed hard, trying not to let the embarrassment consume me.

He lay down on the blanket and propped himself on one elbow. His jacket fell open to show a muscle-hugging T-shirt. It would have been so easy to reach out and trace my fingers over the hills and valleys of his chest, but I didn't.

"I've been here long enough to know that even though you were raised by two parents, your life wasn't pleasant." His position was almost one of protection as he shielded Blue on his side. One of his long fingers traced the train design on Blue's sweater.

"How can I complain when I wasn't starved or beaten or abused regularly? I sound like such a whiner." My childhood had been perfect compared to Ryker's and Silas's.

"You don't have to be beaten to be abused." His eyes brimmed with tenderness and compassion.

"I know, but look at what you went through, and here I sit complaining about my life."

He rolled to his back and looked up at the sky, the sun glinting off his eyes. They were a cross between deep ocean blue and gunmetal gray but edged more toward the blue.

"We each have a different threshold. Our experiences make us who we are."

I also lay on my side and turned toward him. "Who are you, Silas?"

"I'm not sure anymore." He rolled over so Blue was the only thing between us. "I woke up thinking I was one thing, and now I'm not." He reached over and brushed back the hair that had blown in my face.

"You want to talk about it?" I could tell there was something going on with him. A glazed look of despair spread over his face. Without thought, I cupped his cheek. "Talk."

The sadness was replaced by a fleeting smile. "I was hoping I could talk to Blue. He seems to be a good listener."

I ran my hand down Silas's cheek and pinched his chin. "Oh, he is. He's cheap therapy. All he wants is a clean diaper and a full stomach. Blue's a great listener. He never interrupts."

"He probably gets that from his mother." He scooted in so his chest touched Blue's side.

"His mother is a mess," I said, "but she's working on it. That's all we can do. We fall and get up. One door closes, and another one opens. It's the way of life."

His expression stilled and grew serious. "When the door slams in your damn face, what do you do?"

"Find another one to walk through." Blue let out a squeal, and I looked at my watch. It had been hours since he ate. "You hungry, little buddy?" My eyes snapped to Silas when I used his nickname, and what greeted me was a heartwarming smile.

"Can I feed him?"

"You want to feed him?" I sat up and fidgeted in the baby bag for the water and formula. I measured it and shook it while Blue built himself into a frenzied fit.

"I'd like to feed him. If you don't mind." He reached for the bottle and placed it into the baby's rooting mouth. Silas stared at him and shook his head. "Man, you got screwed."

"What are you talking about?" I watched Silas look down at my son, and I wished I could hear what he was thinking.

"Yesterday he got the real deal, and today he's got to suck on a rubber tip. That's bullshit in my book."

The heat of a blush rose to my neck. Were we really talking about my nipples? "Do you think he can tell the difference?"

Silas gave me a look that said, *you can't be serious*. "He's a guy. We start this love of nipples and breasts early." His eyes dropped to my chest, which was covered by a sweater, but might as well have been naked. "You have amazing breasts, by the way."

It had been a long time since anyone had told me I had amazing anything. My mouth widened, and I lifted the corners heavenward. "You were peeking when I was nursing."

His lightning grin made my insides turn to jelly. "Guilty, but not sorry." He slipped the half-drunk bottle from Blue's mouth. "Aren't I supposed to burp him or something?"

I might have fallen in love. For a man who didn't want children, he seemed pretty interested in doing a good job with mine.

"I can do that." I sat up and lifted Blue from the blanket. Silas shifted to a sitting position and held his hands out. "Tell me what to do."

Yep, I was falling, and it was too bad because Silas was everything I would have never considered—which was probably everything I should have.

I showed him how to prop the baby over his shoulder and tap on his back gently. Blue was over eight pounds, which was a decent size for a baby, but against Silas's body, he resembled a preemie—so tiny and frail next to this mountain of a man.

He did this pat-and-rub thing that seemed to work, and when Blue let out a belch to rival a beer drinker's, Silas smiled like he'd accomplished something major. He laid him back onto the blanket and resumed feeding.

"I'm sorry for dragging you into that stupid ploy." I reached down and picked at the fuzzy bits on my sweater.

He gave a shrug. "No apology is necessary. I enjoyed it. Something about being around you and the baby makes me feel at peace somehow."

A skitter of joy raced up my spine and settled in my heart. *Silas Savage may think he doesn't like kids, but judging by the way he looks at*

Blue, he's lying to himself. "If you're ever looking for more peace, I'm always up for some help with watching this little bugger."

To my surprise, he accepted. "How about this Friday? I can bring dinner." He pulled the empty bottle from Blue's mouth as soon as the crinkling sound of the empty plastic bladder filled the air. Up onto his shoulder went Blue, and the pat-and-tap motion began anew. After a series of less-impressive burps, he laid him back down on the soft blue blanket.

"It's a date." I slapped my hand over my lips. *Was it a date?* "I mean ... I didn't assume. It's a figure of speech."

Silas leaned over Blue and touched his mouth to mine. "It's a date," he whispered against my lips before he pulled away. "It's probably time we hung out together, since we're married and everything." The lazy heat of desire glittered in his eyes.

My heart flipped and flopped until it fell into my stomach. I had a date with Silas Savage. My spirits buoyed. My father had walked out of one door of my life, and Silas was walking in another.

It took every ounce of restraint not to lean forward and kiss him again. That pass-by was hardly enough to satisfy. It was enough to make me crave more.

Silas jumped to his feet. "I've got to get that bike back to Ryker." His eyes skated over my body, and a look of regret washed over his face. "Wish I could stay longer."

I jumped up and hand-pressed the wrinkles out of my jeans. "It was nice seeing you, Silas." I packed up Blue's stuff. "I need to be going too. I've got work to do." As a virtual assistant, I did everything from newsletters to advertising. Today was web enhancement for a nutritional supplement company. I had to make a green smoothie look as appetizing as a burger and fries.

I'd come out here to clear my head of all the stressful shit that would sabotage my ability to think. Silas's visit accomplished that, but now my thoughts were full of him. His smile. His touch. His kiss. I would rock that ad because I'd make that damn glass of greens look as appealing as a kiss from Silas, which was way better than a burger and fries.

He helped me pack up the rest, then he leaned over and picked up Blue. I loved the way he held him close to his chest like he was protecting him. I loved the way Blue relaxed in his arms. Oh, hell, I loved that, for at least the moment, I had someone to share my life with.

I knew it wasn't forever, but then again, what was?

CHAPTER 16

SILAS

It was Friday morning, and Ryker and I sat in what was becoming our normal booth at the diner.

"So, you have a date with Grace tonight?" He leaned back and gave me a don't-mess-this-up look. "She's Ana's best friend, so don't screw with her head, okay?"

I sipped my coffee. My date with Grace had been in the forefront of my mind all week. I'd avoided her since that day in the park because I had to wrap my head around the whole situation. She was freaking irresistible, but she was everything I had evaded my whole life.

When I was with her, my broken pieces were glued back together. I was still sharp and jagged and cracked, but somehow, she made me feel whole.

"I'm not planning on hurting her. It's just dinner."

Hannah arrived at the table with the coffee pot. She frowned at Ryker and turned to me. "Did he say date?" Her head tilted that way a girls does when she's proving her point. The point being, she'd told me a few days ago that I wasn't single. Did she see something I wasn't aware of? Women were gifted with magical awareness, along with a bullshit detector and the ability to bust a set of balls with a word or two.

"No, dinner with Grace and Blue." I reached for the sugar packets and pulled two from the container. I didn't usually like my coffee sweet, but ever since I'd drunk Grace's doctored-up coffee that first night, I'd taken a liking to a splash of cream and a dose of sugar.

"Mmm hmm," she hummed.

"What about you? How was the blind date?"

She shuddered from her shoulders to her toes. "He was a weirdo, and he got hands-on if you know what I mean. I socked him in the face and then got out of there."

"Right hook or left?"

She put the coffee pot on the table and lifted her right arm in a Rosie the Riveter pose. "I gave him the right. He deserved more than what my left could offer."

"Thatta girl," I answered. "A man shouldn't take advantage of a woman."

Ryker reached up and squeezed Hannah's flexed muscle. "Or underestimate the power of her right hook."

"You do any damage?" It would serve the asshole right if she blackened his eye.

"Uh, huh." Her head bobbed like a yo-yo. "I bloodied his nose and bruised his pride."

"Right on." We slapped hands together in a high-five.

She topped off our coffee cups and walked away.

"Since when did you and Hannah become friends?" Ryker opened four packets of sugar and dumped them into his mug.

"It's not like we're friends, but I stopped to help her after Junior pulled me over that day I test-drove the Harley." The memory of that day had yet to stop making me smile. The wind in my hair and Grace's lips on mine had made that day one of the best since my return.

"Watch that one." He turned to watch Hannah walk away. "She's a handful."

I could see that. She had an air about her that said she was three parts determination and one part wit. "She's not my handful. That's all I care about."

"Grace seems like a handful too. Not sure whether that's good or bad."

His slight against Grace rubbed me wrong. In my book, Grace was near perfect, but I said nothing because saying something would prove I liked the girl more than I was willing to admit.

"Grace isn't my handful either." There were a lot of handfuls of Grace that I'd like to make mine. A handful of her breasts. A handful of her curvy ass. Yep, I'd like Grace to be my handful, but that was another thing I wasn't 'fessing up to.

"So, I called Henry and told him to continue." Ryker waited, clearly curious to see my reaction. And who could blame him? I'd been all over the place with this subject, from *we've got to find him* to *let him live his life*. I was still mixed on the topic.

"What do you want me to say? Find him if that's what you want. Don't be surprised if he's let down when he meets us."

"I don't know where this whiplash behavior is coming from." His jaw tightened and twitched. "You were insistent months ago, and now you're not. What the hell, Silas?"

"My life is a jumbled mess right now. I've been kicked out of where I want to be and pushed back to a place I never wanted to go. Life is bending me over and asking me to spread my cheeks, so forgive me if I'm a bit twisted on the subject."

"I get it. Life can be a bitch." He sipped his coffee and looked outside like he was remembering all the times his life had turned to shit.

Talk about feeling like an asshole. My brother had done six years in prison for me. I'd do anything to give him back that time, and here I was busting his balls for wanting to find what was rightfully ours. He wanted to find our brother so we could be the family we were supposed to be.

"You know what?" I slapped my hands on the table in total resignation. "I'm sorry. I'm wallowing in my misery."

People depended on me to be present, and I needed to snap out of it. My life was messy, but when hadn't it been? Ryker may have given Ana the nickname Phoenix, but I too had risen from the ashes—at least a hundred times. All I knew was life always went on.

A change was coming. I wasn't sure whether it was my departure from the Army, my move back to Fury, or finding Decker, but it was in the air around me. It crackled like a live wire inside me. That feeling of inevitability that something was happening and all I could do was sit back and let it happen.

And to start that change, I smiled at Ryker and said, "I'm glad Henry is still on the job. He's turned up more than we could have found ourselves. So, now I've got to go to Fort Carson to out-process. Right now I'm burning up leave, but if I go there soon, I can start my terminal leave and cash in my regular leave for pay. That could give us a sizable chunk to put away for future private-eye payments."

Ryker leaned across the booth and punched me in the shoulder. "Yeah man, now you're talking." He sat back with a joker-esque smile. I'd never seen him so pleased.

"We better get that place in shape if he's going to come and visit. He has no reference point for where we lived when he was little, and I'd like to make it nice in case he wants to come here and stay."

Ryker nodded. "Paint and elbow grease go a long way." His whole demeanor had gone from dull to bright. Once we were on the same page, he lit up like a firecracker. "You should have seen Ana's place when she moved in—awful."

"She has a way with damaged goods." My brother had been a prime example of how that woman could change a lump of coal to a diamond.

"Maybe she should work on the house above The Nest."

Ryker tilted his head. "You know The Nest never referred to the garage, right? It was always the house. Mom named it because she wanted all of her chicks to have a nest to return to. People assumed it was the garage because it's where Dad did his work. And we were the War Birds."

I thought on that for a moment. "You're not bullshitting me, are you?"

"No, I remember one day coming home from school and asking her why Dad's club had a sissy name like The Nest when the men had such awesome names like Raptor and Kite and Hawk like mine, and that's what she told me."

"You got the cool name. I got saddled with Rooster."

"I don't know, man—I'm the hawk, and you're the cock. I don't think you fared too poorly."

He was right. Being called Rooster opened lots of opportunity for comedy and conversation. What guy didn't want to talk about his junk, whether in the factual or figurative sense?

Ryker pulled a few bucks out of his wallet. "I've got to be back at the shop so Brick can pick up his bike."

"Brick?" I couldn't figure out what that was supposed to stand for. The guy was either as dense as the name implied or built like a wall. I was hoping the latter.

"Big son of a gun, but nice as can be."

"I'm picking up Mexican food from Domingo's over in Pine Creek. Ana says Grace loves it, and now that she's not nursing, I thought I'd surprise her."

It was obvious by the look on Ryker's face that he knew I dug this girl, but to his credit, he didn't bust my balls about it. "Keep it wrapped, bro, one in diapers at a time is enough." He slid from the booth.

I gave him two thumbs up and said, "No glove, no love."

I tossed a few more singles on the table for Hannah. She wasn't my type, but she wasn't looking for anything more than the rest of us. She wanted to belong.

CHAPTER 17

GRACE

It was a miracle there wasn't a path worn in the hardwood floor. I'd paced the living room for an hour.

I'd made a circle around the coffee table, rearranging the wine bottle and glasses a half dozen times. Was it too much? Did he drink wine?

Each time a car drove down the street, my pulse picked up, and my heart galloped out of my chest.

"Maybe I shouldn't have asked Ana to take the baby," I said to no one. "What if he did only want to help me out with Blue?"

Don't be an idiot, I chastised myself. He looked at me the way a man looked at a woman he wanted, not the way a man looked at a woman whose kid he wanted to help babysit. Or maybe I was so out of practice I didn't know anymore. Pregnancy had a way of killing much-needed brain cells.

Nervous wasn't my modus operandi. In the past, confidence oozed from my pores along with an abundance of sex appeal, but tonight I was more nervous than a virgin at a prison rodeo.

What was it about Silas that made my breath hitch and my heart race? He wasn't the best-looking man I'd seen, and he wasn't the best dressed, but there was a connection and a spark that I couldn't ignore.

I flopped down on the couch and began another conversation with myself. "I hope he buys the idea that Ana had to see Blue, and I hope he won't leave the moment he sees the baby isn't here."

As I was getting ready to talk myself out of this date, a light knock sounded at the door. I took a last glance at myself in the mirror and questioned the lipstick and the dress. But it was too late to change, so I pulled back my shoulders and tried to get in touch with the sexy woman I used to be. Was that only a year ago?

When I opened the door, Silas stood there sexy as hell in faded blue jeans and a black T-shirt that gripped his chest like superglue. In one hand was a takeout bag from Domingo's; in the other was a six-pack of Mexican beer.

"You brought Mexican food." The man would inch his way into my heart one taco at a time.

He stepped inside my living room and walked straight to the kitchen like he belonged here, but then again, he'd been staying at Ana's, and her house was the mirror image of mine. Track homes were the thing when this neighborhood was built.

"I'd like to say I came up with the idea on my own, but Ana told me you loved Domingo's. I hope you like beer too."

In all honesty, I liked anything at this point. After spending the biggest part of the year sober, I'd drink mouthwash if I had to.

"Is Blue sleeping?" He unpacked the bag while I pulled two clean plates from the cupboard.

Here it was, the moment of truth. Did I confess to wanting to have some grown-up time with him, or did I tell the fib I had prepared? Mona's words came back to me: *We all lie, but it's understanding why we lie that's important.* I wouldn't lie to Silas. His life had enough bullshit. He didn't need mine too. "No, I thought it might be nice to have time alone. If you'd rather Blue be with us, I can run down the street and grab him."

One brow quirked up. "Time alone sounds great. How much time do we have?"

"All night." I ducked my head, afraid to see what was written on his face.

"Excellent plan." He piled food on our plates and gripped two beer bottles. They hung from his fingers like bats in a cave dangling back and forth as he walked to the living room.

He set his plate on the table and patted the space on the couch beside him. We sat in silence until he twisted the tops from the beers and handed me one.

He lifted his bottle in a toast. "Here's to closing doors."

"And opening new ones." We tapped bottles and took drinks. The cold bubbles tickled. I'd always been a wine or martini girl, but this beer was as good as a glass of Cristal Champagne.

"What doors did you close, Grace?"

I swallowed a bite of taco. "It's been an eventful week for me. I almost killed my kid with breast milk, so I gave up nursing." I grabbed hold of my boobs and cradled them in my palms. Silas's eyes followed my hands. "You can't imagine how painful the last few days have been with engorged breasts, but I'm doing good now."

"I could have helped you with that." He smiled around his forkful of rice.

"You're a regular hero." I scooped a bite of guacamole with a chip.

His shoulders lifted along with the corners of his beautiful lips. "I do what I can. What else happened this week?"

"My dad disowned me because I'm an unwed mother." I debated telling Silas that Blue's father was my boss but decided that the best road forward was an open road. "And my baby's father was my boss and a married man."

He sat back and sipped his beer.

Fear raced through my cells. Would he judge me like my father?

I rushed out with, "It's the guy I told you about at the bar, the one who didn't tell me he was married," like somehow that would make a difference. The fact was, I was still a single mother with an infant. Not the cream of the crop when it came to desirable single women.

He turned toward me until our knees touched—my soft skin against his rough denim.

"You're not to blame." Warm hands covered mine. "How your father can walk away from you is insane." He leaned forward and brushed one hand over my cheek. "How he can walk away from Blue is unforgivable."

"Coming from the man who doesn't like kids." I leaned into his warm palm and let the heat of his touch soak into me.

"You misunderstood. I never said I didn't like kids. I said I never imagined having any myself." He dropped his hand, and my face felt naked and bare.

"You would make a great father. You've been nothing but wonderful with Blue."

"Blue is easy. He doesn't require much but food."

"You have potential, but I won't try to convince you."

We finished eating, finished the six-pack of beer, and then moved on to the wine.

"You talked of a door slamming the other day. Ready to talk about it?" I pushed the plates to the edge of the table and lifted my feet to the top of the smooth wood surface. It had been a long time since I'd worn heels, and I liked the way they made my legs look. With the way Silas stared, he obviously liked them too.

He shifted closer like he needed to touch me for support. I leaned into his body and set my head on his shoulder. It was comfortable and felt right.

"I've been a special forces soldier for years. It's what I do."

"Impressive and respectable."

He lifted his arm and wrapped it around my shoulder. "Correction. It's what I did."

"Oh." My stomach twisted—for him.

"I've spent more time in Afghanistan in the last decade than out of it. Apparently, the dust and fumes aren't good for the lungs. I've got something they call occupational lung disease or Gulf War syndrome."

"Oh, no. Can they cure it?"

He remained silent for a few minutes. His free hand tapped on his chest. "No, not really. Their way to treat it is to stop the exposure. Since I'm a combat soldier, that means no more combat." A heavy sigh whistled through the air. "I could probably fight it and get a desk job, but they're offering me medical retirement, and my first sergeant says

I should take it." His voice was filled with the kind of sadness you found at funeral homes and cemeteries. Then again, he was burying a piece of himself.

Torn between feeling sad that Silas had lost his job and joy that maybe he would stay, I didn't show a reaction. "What will you do?"

He gripped my chin and turned my head toward him. "I will open another door." His lips pressed against mine. His kiss overflowed with need. In that moment, I was beautiful and desirable and somehow worthy of his attention. I was what he needed, and I was happy to help.

Lips touched lips, and tongues tangled together until we were breathless. He pulled away and nipped on my lower lip until I moaned. He swallowed my sounds with another kiss. One hand threaded through my hair and pulled me closer as if he feared I'd get away.

I wasn't going anywhere. In his embrace, with his mouth on mine, was where I wanted to be. I was tipsy on wine and beer and drunk on passion. My hands clumsily groped for a piece of him, but all I came up with was a handful of his cotton shirt.

In one swift motion, he lifted me to straddle his lap. My dress hiked up to my thighs, and my heels dropped to the floor. Our kiss ended, but the heat and energy that arced between us kept on. My forehead pressed against his, and I dragged in several ragged breaths.

"You're so damn beautiful." He held my hips and pulled me against his hardness. "How are you not someone's?"

"I'm yours if you want me." The words spilled from my kiss-swollen lips.

He lifted his hips to press his arousal against my damp panties. "Baby, this is how much I want you. You ready to open this door?"

Am I? My head screamed *yes*. My heart screamed *yes*. My body screamed *hell yes*.

"Yes," I whispered. "Take the wine and yourself to my room. Second door on the right. I'll be right in."

His hands moved to cup my face. "This doesn't have to happen. It may be too soon for you."

Silas was an enigma; he sent out this tough-as-nails vibe, but he was a softy. I rocked against his erection and laughed to myself. Not exactly soft there.

My lips pressed to his one more time before I slid from his lap. Once I pushed the half-full bottle of Merlot and glasses into his hand, I turned him in the right direction and propelled him forward. I needed a moment to come to terms with what I was about to do.

CHAPTER 18

SILAS

The candle that I found next to the bed flickered and cast shadows of light on the white walls. I watched the prisms dance while I waited for Grace. She went from the kitchen to the bathroom where she turned the water on and off no less than a dozen times.

Stripped naked and lying beneath the floral bedspread that smelled like her, I waited. She was sweet and flowery and feminine. A nice change from the sweat and funk I'd faced each day in the desert.

My hands glided across the soft sheets. The queen bed pleased me. You could lose track of your lover in a king-sized bed, and you could smother each other to death in a twin or a full. This was perfect. Every moment I spent with her was perfect.

"Grace, you okay?" I called out.

"Yes, I'll be right there." Her voice quivered, and I knew she was on the verge of locking herself in the bathroom and not coming out.

"Come out here. You don't have to be afraid."

She mumbled something I couldn't hear and then appeared in the doorway. Her dress was gone. In its place was a pink robe held together by a tightly pulled sash.

"What's wrong, Grace?"

"Nothing." She tugged at the tie until I knew it cinched her waist uncomfortably.

I tapped the bed beside me. "Come here." The bedspread sat at my waist, and her eyes didn't leave my bare chest.

"You have a tattoo."

My hand went to the ink on my chest. "I got it on my eighteenth birthday."

"A clock?" She leaned against the doorjamb and stared at the ink. "Why a clock?"

"A reminder that we only have the moment we're in. What do you want in this minute, Grace?" It was odd for her to be standing in the doorway while I was tucked in her bed.

"I want you." The sexy purr of her voice made me want to jump out of bed and toss her over my shoulder.

"I'm here." I spread my arms and hoped she'd climb into them.

"Silas, I'm not … I had a baby." She rubbed her hands over her hips and then her stomach.

"Oh, my God, Grace. Really? I thought the stork dropped him off on your porch."

"Don't make fun of me, Silas. I'm having a moment here—an insecure moment—and you're not helping."

"Sweetheart, let's get this out of the way."

"What?"

"Tell me everything you think is wrong with you, but come here first." I rubbed the spot on the mattress beside me.

She looked at me and looked at the bed. She warred within herself, and I felt like I was on the losing edge. At this point, I didn't give a shit if we slept together; all I wanted was to hold her and be close to her.

There was a fifty-fifty chance she'd bolt. To my surprise, she didn't. Instead, she made her way to the side of the bed, and when she was within arm's length, I tugged the belt of her robe and pulled her to me.

"Tell me."

She pulled her beautiful plump lower lip between her teeth and gnawed. "My breasts—"

"Are perfect." I pulled the edge of her robe open until her breasts fell free. My hands cupped them, and my thumbs brushed over her nipples, which pebbled on contact.

She hissed through her teeth. A damn sexy sound that meant my touch excited her. When my lips hit her rosy pink nipples, she let out a moan that made my rod stand at attention. I pulled away, letting her nipple pop from my mouth.

"Poor Blue. He's stuck with that rubber shit, and I've got these." I kissed the top of each breast and sat back. "What else?"

She looked down at her silk-covered stomach. "Well … I have stretch marks."

I tugged the tie and let the soft silky robe fall open. My hand went to her tummy. "These aren't stretch marks. They're battle scars." I leaned forward and showed her the burn scar on my shoulder and the knife wound on my back. "Do you like me less because of these?"

"No, but you earned those in battle."

I laughed, not at her, but at the silliness of her concerns. "Honey, I'd say that you battled your way through pregnancy. Did you have morning sickness?"

She nodded.

"Swollen feet?"

"Yes." Her smile proved that she knew what I was getting at.

"Back pains? Leg cramps?"

"Yes."

"How long were you in labor?" I knew enough about pregnancy to know it wasn't a walk in the park. Many of my soldiers had wives and kids, and their stories were enough to keep a man celibate.

"Fourteen hours."

"Okay, so I've been shot and knifed and burned, but I've never pushed a six-pound baby out of my junk, and sweetheart, I never want to. The medal of valor goes to you." My hands caressed her thighs until my thumbs reached her lacy underwear. I skimmed under the elastic and watched her eyes close as my roughened fingertips brushed against her velvet skin.

"That's the other thing. I had a six-pound baby come out of me, and I'm not sure …"

That was enough of her insecurities. "Grace, lie down." I didn't give her any options but to do what I said. I flipped her over my lap and pressed her to the mattress. "You are a damn beautiful woman, and I plan on enjoying every inch of your body."

She lay on her back, and I straddled her hips. My throbbing rod bounced against her belly. I traced the two lines she worried about. They angled like a V with one line on each side of her stomach. "It's like an arrow pointing me to your treasure." I traced the fading red lines until I hit the edge of her panties. "These have to go, Grace." I lifted and tugged them down her long sexy legs.

She was neat and trimmed, and only the lightest patch of soft red hair covered her sex. I leaned down and slid my tongue along the slit. Her tense legs fell open as I settled between her thighs.

She tasted sweet and savory. Sugary and salty. She was perfect. "God, I love this."

Her hands tried to grip my short hair, but there wasn't much to grab on to, so she palmed my head and pulled my lips tight against her sex. I probed the seam of her slick heat until she moaned, and then I pulled her tight bundle of nerves into my mouth and rolled my tongue across it. Her hips bucked while I sucked and nipped at her. And when her muscles tensed, I moved away.

She rose to her elbows and gave me a look that could pierce my skin. "Don't stop. What's wrong with you?"

The best thing about her irritation was she was no longer thinking about her perceived deficiencies. All she was thinking about was her pleasure. It was about time we were on the same page.

"Lie back and enjoy, Grace. I'm going to love on you like you've never been loved on before."

I climbed up her body and let my heavy length rest between her legs. There was nothing I wanted more than to press into her, but Grace needed to understand that tonight was about more than sex. I was opening a door that I intended to keep open. This was a big deal for me. This wasn't a one-and-done. This was more. It should have scared the hell out of me, but it didn't. I had come to terms with my life. I'd lost my job and gained a companion. I had no idea where this would go, but I knew I'd give her nothing less than my best.

What started with a kiss quickly turned into me moving down her body. After I teased her nipples and tasted her skin, my lips went back to the place she wanted them—on her clit. I sucked and savored her. She was hot and slick, and when her knees shook, I didn't have the heart to pull away even though I wanted to prolong our first experience.

One finger pressed into the hot velvet of her sex while I pulled her swollen button between my lips. She moaned and groaned and ground her sex into my face.

"God, Silas. Sooo good." Her words made my groin ache.

I probed her tight channel with a single finger. If I didn't know better, I would have called her a liar about the six-pound baby.

"You're so damn tight."

"You're such a good liar," she panted.

I pressed a second finger inside, and her body quaked. My fingers stroked her insides as my tongue stroked her outside. Her hands gripped the sheets as her thighs pressed against my head.

"Oh, God. Oh, God. Oh, God," she cried out as her body shuddered and her insides fluttered around my fingers. I drew every last quiver from her body before I pulled away.

When I looked up at her, she was sprawled out on the bed. Gone was the worry that had furrowed her brow. Gone was the frown that pulled her smile down. In its place was a glowing, beaming woman, and she was looking between my legs. We weren't done.

As much as I wanted to ride her bare, I'd never do that to her. I grabbed the condom I'd set on the nightstand and rolled it onto my length.

"That's quite a rooster," she teased.

I lined up to her entrance. "I'm the Rooster, baby, and this is my cock-a-doodle-doo." I pressed inside her, and my entire world went silent. My brain, heart, and body were all in sync for one perfect moment, and the only thought that came to mind was that Grace Faraday was mine.

She pulled her legs up and wrapped them around my waist. "Damn perfection," I groaned.

I didn't take her hard, although I had every intention of doing that later. This time it was slow and loving because that's what we both needed. Grace needed to know that she was more than a quick lay. I needed to know that she wasn't going anywhere. Each time I sank myself inside her, I screamed the word *mine* in my head. Life hadn't been fair to me. It had taken everything from my parents to my innocence. Surely the universe would allow me to keep Grace as a gift for having survived.

CHAPTER 19

GRACE

He slept like the dead. His hand sat heavy on my hip, and when I turned toward him, it fell with a thump to the bed, but he remained asleep.

His thick lashes fluttered against his cheeks as puffs of air separated his lush lips with each breath. My fingers traced the scruff on his face, coarse black hairs that had left a delicious burn between my thighs.

I dropped to his chest and outlined the clock inked in blacks and grays. I'd commented that it was backward, and he'd corrected me: When he stared in the mirror, it was perfect. The hands were set to 3:36, the time his life changed forever.

Time was a funny thing, and his tattoo was a reminder that we didn't have an infinite number of minutes in our lives. How much time would I have with Silas? Forever wasn't something I had considered until he pressed himself inside me. For the first time in my life, I'd felt perfection.

Inquisitive fingers ran down his chest and skimmed over the scars of a rough life. The silver lines reminded me that Silas had fought for everything he had.

When I dragged my gaze up his body, his blue-gray eyes were open. He greeted me with a smile and a raspy, sleepy hello.

His hands skimmed over my flesh, his calloused fingertips stopping in places he knew turned me on. The sensitive area beneath my breasts, my tender nipples, the spot where my collarbone met my neck, the lobe of my ear, my lips.

"Did you get enough sleep?" His blue eyes searched mine for the truth.

"I never get enough sleep, but I'm getting used to it." With Blue reaching the two-month mark, he was sleeping more, but I never got more than four consecutive hours. "You were a far better alternative to sleep." I pressed a soft kiss to his lips. "Do you want coffee?"

He nodded, and I moved to get up, but his hand lowered to my hip and pulled me close to him. There was no question about what else he wanted.

I was sore in all the right places, but I didn't care. Until Silas, I was convinced I'd die single and alone with a latex penis and pack of D batteries.

He twisted around to look at the single remaining condom. Yep, we'd used four last night.

"How about I have you first and then I make the coffee?"

His plan was appealing, but I had to rescue Ana and Ryker from Blue. "I have to get the baby."

He turned over and picked up his phone. His fingers danced over the screen, and seconds later, I could hear the muted ring.

"Hey, bro, is Blue okay?"

A quiet male voice said something I couldn't hear.

"Can you give us another hour? I'll buy breakfast."

There was more muffled conversation on the other end before Silas said, "Thanks, man."

He tossed his phone on the nightstand and picked up the condom. "Blue is fine. Where were we?"

There was nothing like morning sex. An orgasm or two could do a body good—it got your heart pumping and your adrenaline racing to start the day. Add to that a hot-as-hell man who wanted to please you and then bathe you after, and you pretty much had nirvana. And it wasn't even nine in the morning.

Hand in hand, we walked down to Ana and Ryker's house. When we entered, Ana had Blue cradled in her arms, feeding him. Silas went straight to my little boy.

"Do you mind? I like to feed him." He held out his arms and waited for Ana to hand Blue over.

She quirked one brow skyward and relinquished him right away. "I'll get cleaned up, and we can go to breakfast. I hear Silas is buying."

He didn't pay one ounce of attention to her. Silas sat in the old leather chair and cradled my son in his arms while he fed him. It would've been a damn Norman Rockwell moment if he were alive and painting bad boys caught in soft moments. Ana stopped in the doorway and gave me her I'm-happy-for-you smile.

Life comprised seconds and minutes and hours and days, but it was the seconds you needed first because without them there were no minutes or hours or … I watched Silas feed Blue, and I knew in that second, I was the happiest woman in the world. My life was good, my body was sated, and my heart felt full.

I walked over and sat on the arm of the chair and looked down at Blue. He stared up into Silas's eyes like he was looking at a superhero. His mouth opened around the bottle, and I swore he was smiling. Not the smile a baby gets when they're gassy or fill their pants, but a genuine happy smile.

Silas shifted, then patted and rubbed Blue's back until he got the response he wanted, and now that I'd had those hands on me, I could see why he was so effective. Silas dove into everything with enthusiasm because he understood the value of seconds and minutes and hours.

Fifteen minutes later, we had piled into Ana's Jeep and arrived at the diner. Hannah brought three cups of regular coffee and a cup of decaffeinated for Ana, but no menus—we'd become such regulars that we didn't need them. She ignored Ryker and smiled down at Silas and me.

"Told you," she said smugly before taking our order.

After Hannah strutted off to the kitchen to place our order, I turned toward Silas with a tilt to my head. "She told you what?"

"That I wasn't single when I thought I was."

I had no idea what he was talking about. "Care to elaborate?"

Ryker stepped into the conversation. "Everyone saw the spark between you two but you. Even Not-So-Happy Hannah recognized what was happening, and she's pretty self-involved."

I looked toward the kitchen to the blonde-haired woman who leaned against the counter and picked at the polish on her nails. "She's young. She can't be over twenty-one." It had been a long year for me, and I swore it made me feel more like thirty than the twenty-six years I was.

I turned to Silas. "How old are you?" I'd slept with the man but knew little about him except that I liked him—a lot.

"I just turned twenty-seven. Two years younger than that guy." He nodded toward his brother. "Our birthdays are all in the same month. Mom and Dad apparently loved the month of July for conceiving because all three of us were born in March. Ryker on the 21st, me on the 27th, and Decker on the 31st."

"Aries," I blurted out. I'd gone through a zodiac phase for a month or two. "Hard-headed and stubborn." I looked between the two and nodded. "Sounds about right."

"What are you?" Silas asked.

Ana and Ryker sat back and listened. They had long ago passed these first hurdles in their relationship.

"Valentine's baby," I said with pride. "Not everyone can claim Cupid as their father."

Ana snorted and choked on her coffee. "Saying your father is like Cupid is like comparing a toad to a prince. It can't be done."

"Aquarius. Intelligent, quick-witted and rebellious." Silas talked like an expert on the subject. "This guy in my squadron had a thing for astrology. He was born in February and never missed a chance to tell me he was a smart, funny badass."

"Speaking of your squadron, what's the plan?" Ryker asked.

All eyes turned to Silas.

"I don't have to go back to the desert." His faint smile held a touch of sadness. "They're packing my stuff and shipping it back." He shrugged with indifference, but I knew he felt deeply about the loss of his career. "I'm heading down to Colorado Springs this week. I can out-process at Fort Carson."

I laid my hand on his thigh and gave him a supportive squeeze. When his hand covered mine, I felt something pass through us. We were in this together.

Two days ago, Silas had been out of the question; Mr. I'm Not Having Any Kids sat at the bottom of the eligible-bachelor file. But now he was at the top of the list. Not only was he wonderful with Blue, but he also had other talents that couldn't be overlooked. Sweet, sexy and hella good in bed, Silas Savage was perfection.

CHAPTER 20

SILAS

Poked and prodded and paper-worked to death, I plowed through my medical release. The only thing that kept me sane all week was my regular evening calls with Grace. It was like she was here holding my hand, and that made it easier to let go.

When they'd said I had to retire, I had thought about a life full of nothing, but that was so far from the truth.

Fury had dealt me some shitty blows, and yet it had brought Ana to Ryker and Grace to me. And as much as I thought I didn't want children, I was falling hard and fast for Blue. In a few short days, the kid had me wrapped around his finger.

I'd spent an hour in Babies "R" Us picking out things he'd grow in to like cars, and trucks, and Whoopee cushions.

That toy was my favorite. I'd always loved to put the cushion under an unsuspecting victim, which was usually my mom. She was unfailingly a good sport about it. Her hand would cover her mouth and she'd say, "excuse me." Then she'd pull the rubber bladder from under her bottom and chuck it at me.

For the first time, I was thinking about a future that included Little League games and birthday parties and Christmases—stuff I'd never considered before Grace and Blue.

I stopped at the florist and picked up flowers. I'd never purchased flowers for anyone in my life, and I had no idea what she'd like, so I got a bunch of everything and made the three-hour drive home. If it hadn't been a six-hour round trip, I would have been in Grace's bed every night. The three days I had spent there before I left for Fort Carson were the best I'd had in a lifetime.

When I pulled into her driveway, she rushed out of the door and flung herself into my arms.

"You're home." She peppered my face with what seemed like a thousand kisses, and it wasn't enough. "I missed you so much."

"I missed you too." I gripped her ass and pulled her up until she wrapped her legs around my waist. "It scares me how much I missed you." I covered her mouth with mine and relished the taste of her and the feel of her in my arms.

I needed her, and that was scarier than walking through a minefield, which I'd done several times. A minefield could take you out with one wrong step. Failing at love could be much more painful. It was ongoing hurt that reminded you that you were unlovable, which was why I'd erected a wall around my heart years ago. But this woman was chipping at that barrier every day with her love and affection. Add in a fatherless boy, and I was a goner.

"Are you home for good?" She unwrapped her legs and slid down my body.

Home. This was home for me now. It wasn't Fury. It wasn't Ryker. It was this fiery green-eyed redhead who had worked her way into my head and my heart.

"I'm home to stay." I reached into the car and pulled out an armful of flowers and handed them to her.

"Silas Savage, who knew you were a romantic?" She brought them to her nose and breathed in their fresh sweet scent. All the way up here I had smelled them, and they reminded me of Grace's perfume.

"I'm working on it." I shut the door to Ryker's car, thinking I'd have to get my own ride soon. "Where's my little buddy?"

Grace looked over her shoulder toward the front door. "I just put

SAVING SILAS

him down for a nap." There was a sexy glint in her eye and a knowing smile on her face.

"So, we have an hour?" I was already pulling her to the house.

"At least, maybe two if we're quiet and lucky."

I rushed her straight to the bedroom. "I'm feeling pretty damn lucky."

She wasted no time in stripping my clothes off and pushing me down on the mattress. That was what I loved about Grace. She was one part angel and three parts she-devil. She knew what she wanted, and apparently, right now it was me in her mouth.

The minute she pulled my length into the hot wet recesses and swirled her tongue around the sensitive tip, I was lost. "What are you doing to me?" I groaned. My fingers threaded through her long red hair and followed the up-and-down movements as she swallowed my length.

"I'm loving on you," she whispered against the tip. The vibration from her words nearly sent me over the edge.

"I'm loving your loving." Grace had serious talents in the bedroom department. I didn't dwell on how she became so skilled at pleasing me. I didn't care. Neither one of us was a saint.

"I have a surprise for you." She slid from the bed and rose to her feet. With the hem of her T-shirt in her hands, she pulled it up and lifted it over her head.

I stared at her pink lacy bra and grinned. "I like it." She might have worn that for me, but what I wanted was under that strip of fabric—her little surprise would be gone in seconds. Then she pulled off her pants to show matching pink underwear. I couldn't exactly call them underwear since there was little more than a string and strip of fabric, but I liked them too.

"When's the last time you went bare?" She nipped at her own upper lip while she crawled back between my legs.

"Umm … Umm." How was I supposed to focus when she deep-throated me? I gripped a handful of her hair and stopped her motion. "I can't think."

She pulled her lips off me with a pop and wiped the saliva that pooled in the corner of her mouth. "You don't have to think. You need to feel good."

I pulled her up my body until she lay on my chest. He hair smelled like citrus, and her skin smelled like lavender. "You make me feel so good, Grace, and I'm not talking about the sex. I feel normal when I'm with you."

"You are normal." She reached her hands behind her back and unlatched the hooks of her bra. Soft globes spilled from the cups onto my chest. She sat up and straddled me. My length sat squarely between her legs. My hands reached for the lush curves of her breasts.

She covered my hands with hers and showed me how she liked her nipples rolled between my fingers. She ground that strip of fabric between her legs against me until we were both soaked from her arousal.

"How long, Silas?" Her breath was as labored as mine. Her desire ratcheted up to explosive levels.

"I don't know, Grace, like two years or so." I lifted my hips to get more friction. "It was a stupid thoughtless moment, but nothing came out of it. Why?"

"I want nothing coming between us, Silas. I want you inside of me."

My heart hammered in my chest. The beat pulsed through me like a gun on rapid fire. "Grace—"

"I got the shot. It's effective right now. We can be as close as ever, or we can still keep that barrier between us. It's your call."

Holy shit ... She got the shot for me. For us. There was only one call to make, and that was to flip her over and get rid of that piece of damp pink fabric that blocked my entrance to heaven.

"Are you sure?" I knew Grace had gifted her bare self to one other man, and I wanted to be worthier than him.

She reached forward and lined my length up with her opening. "I've never felt so sure about anything."

I didn't thrust inside of her. I wanted the feeling of her gift to wash over us. I pressed inside with a slow and gentle force. Every damn nerve ending came alive, and with every inch I buried inside her, a piece of me went with it. And the empty spaces left behind from years of sorrow and loss were filled up with the pieces she put inside me. I lost track of where I ended and she began. We were melded together by want and need and something far stronger than both. As silly as it all seemed, I was falling in love with Grace Faraday. In a brief time, she had become as necessary as the air that I breathed and the blood that pumped through my veins. Grace had become everything.

"You're mine, Grace." I hovered over her body, thrusting gently inside.

Her nails skimmed my back. Her eyes pierced my soul. "I'm yours, Silas."

We made slow deliberate love to each other. No other promises were made, no other words spoken. Just the coming together of two hearts and two souls.

Grace got up before me to shower and dress.

I teetered between sleep and a twilight state of bliss until I heard her voice rise in anger: "He doesn't belong to you. Get out."

CHAPTER 21

SILAS

I was used to thirty seconds of prep time, and I'd been trained to act on a second's notice. So when Grace raised her voice, I hopped out of bed and straight into my jeans.

My feet couldn't take me down the short hallway fast enough. I stopped at the sight of a tall blond man standing in the living room. He stood over Grace, threatening her.

Grace's eyes were like those of a trapped wild animal.

"Get out," she hissed between clenched teeth.

I raced into the living room half naked and ready to do battle.

"Who the hell are you?" the man asked, looking at me.

I walked up next to Grace and wrapped my arm around her. "I'm someone you don't want to mess with. If Grace wants you out of her house. I'd suggest you turn the hell around and walk away."

The man took a step back, but I could tell he wasn't going anywhere.

"You know how to pick them, don't you, Grace?" He looked at me like I was the burnt unsavory bit at the bottom of a bag of theater popcorn.

"She asked you to leave." Endorphins kicked in the same way they did when I went on a mission. Everything came into focus. Adrenaline raced through my veins like a dose of mainlined heroin. My lungs tightened, making me realize the Army was right to let me go. I couldn't take on a group of enemy combatants, but I could take on an arrogant asshole.

He stood there and measured me up. That he still stood inside the house meant he'd calculated wrong.

"I want to see my son."

My gut clenched at his words. He was Blue's father. My little man, Blue.

Grace took a step toward the man. "You don't have a son, Trenton. You gave up that right when you told me to abort him." She pushed at his chest. "Get out of my house."

"Your father said he was at risk living with you." The asshole looked at me and my tattoos like I was the risky part.

"My father is delusional. Blue is fine."

"Blue? You named my son Blue?"

Grace looked like she was ready to claw his eyes out. She wouldn't have to. I'd pluck them out with my fingertips without a second thought if the asshole didn't leave.

I rubbed her shoulders and pulled her back a step.

"I named my son Blue. You don't have a son. Go back to the wife no one knew you had."

"She left me. Which is why I'm here. I thought maybe we could—"

I didn't like the way he looked at Grace like he could gobble her up. "Could what, asshole? Play house again?" I stepped in front of Grace to shield her from his eyes. "She's playing house with me, and that boy in there—" I pointed down the hallway. "—he's mine too."

Grace's hand gripped my belt loop and tugged me back. "I've got this." She turned toward me and pleaded with her beautiful eyes. "I can handle this."

I had to give her the space she needed, so I nodded and walked to the kitchen. I fixed a cup of coffee and stood in the doorway where I watched the asshole try to sweet-talk Grace into another chance.

"Grace, we were good together, and now we have a baby." He looked at me when he made that comment. His gaze took in the house that was exactly Grace. "This isn't you. Come back to Denver. I'll put you up in a decent apartment."

The back of her neck turned as red as her hair. She was on fire on the inside, and it was bursting through her skin.

"Oh, you want to put me up in a sweet little apartment? Not your house? What about marriage?" She gave me a quick glance that I knew was her way of saying *watch this*.

The man turned a pale color that resembled death. A shallow chalky color. "I'm not, umm, divorced yet. So, I'd have to keep you …" His words faded.

"Hidden?" she asked pointedly.

"It's not like that. It's complicated." His eyes went to the floor, to me, to Grace. It didn't seem like the man knew who to look at anymore.

"She caught you with another woman. No surprise there, but why show up here?"

"Because your father said my son was in danger." The asshole glared at me. "And I can see he's right."

"What's your end game, Trenton? I didn't ask you for a damn thing but a severance package, which didn't cost you a dime. What do you want from me?"

"I want to know my son."

Territorial wasn't even the right word for what I felt. Blue wasn't his son.

"DNA doesn't make you a daddy," I said. "You know anything about babies?"

"I can learn."

I nodded my head. "How many ounces of water go into a scoop of formula? What's Blue allergic to? What's the one position that calms him down when he's upset?" I knew all of these things, but this asshole thought he had more rights than I did because his sperm survived the trek to the egg. "You value your sleep?"

Trenton stared with his jaw hanging open. "I get enough sleep."

"Now, but Blue would change that. He wakes up for feeding and diaper changes and reassurance. Are you going to be there, or are you going to tap Grace on the ass and say, 'The baby's crying'?" The thought of anyone tapping Grace on the ass infuriated me.

"I can handle it."

I stepped toward him, and he stepped back. *Smart man.* "You think? Maybe you should take him for a weekend to make sure. You know, like test-driving a car. Sometimes you think the Honda will be fine, and then you realize that it's not as smooth of a ride as you thought."

"He is not test-driving my baby." Grace stared at me. "Have you lost your mind?"

Trenton stood as tall as he could. "I'm up for a test drive as long as I get to ride Grace again."

My fist hit his face so fast it startled me.

Grace threw herself between us. I wasn't sure whether she was protecting him or trying to save me.

"This is too good!" Trenton said as he wiped the blood from his cracked lip. "It's like you're trying to make this easy for me. I'll see you in court, Grace."

The second she slammed the door, she was in my face. "What the hell were you thinking?"

"He crossed the line, Grace." A drop of blood dripped from my hand to the hardwood floor.

"How could you be stupid enough to attack him? He's rich. He's got friends in high places, and now you hit him in my house. The house where Blue lives too."

"I protect what's mine, and minutes ago you told me you were mine. Has that changed?"

She pulled my hand up and looked at my bloody knuckles. The skin must have split when it connected with his tooth.

"Come here." She pulled me into the kitchen and doctored my cut. "I'm yours, Silas, but I have to protect Blue first. Surely you understand that."

I pulled her against my chest and let the tension go on an exhale. "I understand better than you think." Once I cleaned up the blood from the living room floor, I sat next to Grace on the couch. "Understand that I've lived my entire life watching people either take abuse or give it. Ryker took beating after beating for me. I paid my share in bruises and blood too."

"I know you understand, but I don't want to stir the pot and cause Trenton to come after me. He won't use his fists. He'll use the legal system to beat me to a pulp."

I pulled her into my lap. "I understand that too. Ryker went to jail for me, and I'll never be able to repay that debt. He killed a man for me, and I'd do the same for anyone I loved. Do you understand what I'm telling you, Grace?"

"Yes, you protect what's yours." She dropped her head to my shoulder.

"You and Blue are mine, Grace. I will take care of you." I pressed my lips against hers. "I love you, Grace." How afraid I was to say those words and yet how easily they fell from my lips.

"I love you too, Silas. Just don't go to jail for me. I'd never be able to live with myself." She wrapped her arms around my waist and squeezed.

"I know what that feels like too." I hadn't forgiven myself or the system for putting my brother away when all he'd done was save me from a lifetime of physical and sexual abuse. I'd considered a thousand ways to repay the debt. None of them were adequate. I'd never saddle Grace with that guilt.

CHAPTER 22

GRACE

It had been a week since Trenton showed up on my porch, and in that time, I'd left about fifty messages for my father. What father does what he did to me?

He had finally responded to one of my voicemails and said he'd meet me at the diner. So there I was, watching Blue's eyes dance from toy to toy that hung from his carrier handle.

Silas had wanted to come with me, but I'd persuaded him to help Ryker at the garage. Business had been picking up since I created a website for them, and while Ryker was keeping up with the motorcycle repairs, the books were a mess. That was something Silas had the skills to do, so he was taking over as business manager.

The bell above the door rang, and Hannah rushed in, looking pale and scared. She glanced at me and ran into the back room.

A few minutes later, she came out looking more like herself but still harried.

"You okay?" I asked. Now that she'd gotten over the idea that the Savage boys were taken, she'd been a lot more pleasant to hang out with. At this point, I'd even call her a friend.

She approached, tying her apron around her waist. "Men can be such assholes."

"You got that right, sister. Who's the asshole this time?"

"Some guy who won't take no for an answer. I don't understand how men haven't been extinguished through natural selection."

I glanced out the window and watched my dad approach the diner. "Speaking of assholes, here comes my dad. Can you bring us two cups of coffee?"

"Sure thing," she said, "give me a wink if you need me to bring out Rusty's bat from the back room."

The bell rang above the door, and my dad looked around the diner for me. He found me right away and slid into the booth across from me without giving Blue a passing glance. I wondered if that was how disconnected he'd been with me during my early years.

"I'm only here, Grace, so you'll stop calling me fifty times a day." He picked up his napkin and folded it into a neat square.

"I only called you fifty times this week. I wouldn't have called you at all except I need to know why you would track down Trenton Kehoe, tell him an outright lie, and then give him my address." I reminded myself to breathe. I looked left to Hannah, who mimicked the swing of a bat before she poured two cups of coffee and started our way.

"You're like your mom."

I couldn't suppress the roll of my eyes. Lord, I'd heard that phrase a million times over. "Why now, Dad?" He'd spent my whole life comparing me to my mother. If sadness consumed me, it was because I had her weak disposition. If happiness filled me, it was because I had her reckless spirit.

"You had a baby, and you didn't even let the father know."

I pounded my fist on the table, jarring the cups of coffee that Hannah had dropped off. I leaned into the center of the table so the whole diner didn't have to hear what I had to say. "First off, he didn't want the baby. He told me to abort it. Not him or her—*it*. Second, what in the hell does that have to do with Mom?"

Dad sipped his black coffee and stared at me. Every few seconds his eyes moved to the baby carrier next to me. "Your mom ruined our relationship. She made me out to be the bad guy all the time, and that's exactly what you'll do when Blue grows up and asks about his father."

I raised my palms to the sky. "What are you talking about? I won't lie to Blue. I'll tell him the truth."

"What is the truth? That you had sex with a married man, got knocked up, and kept him when his father told you to abort him?"

It didn't sound all that appealing when he put it that way, but I would be honest with my son. "Yes, Dad, I'll tell him the truth."

"The truth makes Trenton Kehoe look like an asshole." He dropped a spoon into his coffee and stirred. It made little sense since he added nothing to stir into his black coffee. Maybe that was Dad's gift. He excelled at stirring. Stirring up trouble and stirring up shit.

"Trenton Kehoe is an asshole. He pretended he wasn't married. He took as big of a risk as I did when he didn't wear a condom. I stepped up to the plate, and he stepped out of the stadium. What does this have to do with Mom?"

"He's trying to make amends, and you're punishing him for making a wrong decision. Your mom did the same thing." He pulled the spoon from his coffee and laid it on the folded napkin square.

"Oh. My. God. This is not the same." The dark liquid bled across the white napkin, marring the pristine white of the paper. "You're punishing me because Mom punished you?"

"She turned you against me." Dad clenched his jaw and stared at me.

"Listen to yourself. She didn't turn me against you. You did that yourself. You were an absentee father. You were never home. Your family was the church. You didn't raise me. Mom didn't raise me. I raised myself." I wanted to reach across the booth and give him a V8-commercial-style slap to the forehead, but instead, I took a deep breath.

"I tried to make amends, Grace. Yes, I cheated on your mother like Trenton cheated on his wife. It happens, and then you do what you can to make peace with it, but your mother ... she never let it go."

"And so now you're trying to right your sin by guiding Trenton on how to mend his? What was your plan, Dad? Get him to fight for custody, mend his marriage, and help him take my son away?"

"No, Grace, I don't want him to regret not being with his son. I regret not being with you."

I tossed Blue's things into the diaper bag and prepared to leave. "You know what? You're a hypocrite. You sit here and talk about him missing his son—a son he never wanted—and now you lament about having missed me. That was on you, Dad. We were home waiting. Where were you?"

He dropped his head into his hands, and his shoulders shook. "I was hiding behind my deacon's robes."

I wanted to choke him and hug him at the same time. "While you cleaned and pressed and paraded around in that vestment, I grew up. Mom didn't keep me away from you. You kept yourself away from me because seeing me made you feel farther away from her. Religion should help you face your life, not hide from it."

When he lifted his head, his eyes were red and watery. "I'm sorry, Grace."

I had a moment of clarity where everything made sense. I'd been what some would call promiscuous. I'd tried and tested lots of men. No one ever meshed with me because I wasn't looking for what they were, which was a few minutes naked between the sheets. I needed more. I wanted a place to belong—a place where I could be loved for me. Not the deacon's daughter. Not the hot girl at the bar. Not the sexy assistant. I'd been looking for someone to tell me I was perfect the way I was, and I'd found him in Silas.

My dad's remorseful expression could sway the least forgiving soul. "I'm sorry too, Dad, because what you did with Trenton Kehoe might end up ruining me and my life with Blue. I could lose him because of your interference." I looked down at the sweet baby who had fallen asleep while his mother sorted out the mess she called her life.

"That wasn't my intent." He looked at me, and when the hurt in my eyes became too much for him to handle, he turned his head and looked out the window.

"Stop lying to yourself, Dad. In my living room, you told me I should have given him to someone who would raise him right." I swiped at the tears that rushed from my eyes. "I may not be able to give him everything. I may not be a perfect parent, but at least I love him more than I love myself, and in my book, that's all he needs. I'll figure out the rest."

"Trenton told me there was a man with you. Was that Silas?" His voice rose with something that sounded like hope.

"Yes, Dad. We're important to Silas. He's important to me. We're figuring it all out."

Dad nodded his head. "I like Silas, Grace. He's not who I'd expect you to choose. He's different."

"He's the kind of man who will do whatever it takes to make things right. He's not a peacock, Dad, he's a rooster."

My dad didn't understand what any of that meant, but I did. Silas was the exact opposite of everyone I'd ever desired, and that made him perfect.

I left my dad in the booth to think about what he had done to me. I wasn't sure we would ever have a relationship. The lies about his past had created a problem for my future, and I wasn't certain I could ever forgive him. All I knew was that there was a sexy man who promised to be home at noon, and I planned to be there because what I needed most was someone to tell me it would be okay. Silas was that man.

When I arrived at my house, I found two things I was unprepared for. One was Mr. Chambers sitting in my living room drinking a beer with Silas. The second was a summons from the District Court of Denver to discuss the paternity of Blue Faraday.

CHAPTER 23

SILAS

Grace walked in with Blue cradled in one arm, the mail in one hand, and a frown on her beautiful face.

"Hey, sweetheart," I said as I rose to greet her. "You know Mr. Chambers, right?" The old man was sitting in the red upholstered chair.

She gave him a disgruntled look and nodded her head. "Oh, yes, Mr. Chambers and I are well acquainted." Her tone was clipped and flippant as if she didn't like the man, which I couldn't understand. He was a man's man, and he had amazing war stories to share.

"He's a war hero. Did you know?" I took Blue from her arms and sat on the couch.

"Shocking since he does so poorly on the front line of life." Grace unpacked the baby bag with vigor. It was like she was angry at the bottles and diapers she tossed into untidy piles in the entryway.

The baby looked up at me and gnawed on his fist. "Are you hungry, buddy?"

"I'll get a bottle ready," Grace offered. She looked at Mr. Chambers and narrowed her eyes. "We'd hate for him to do what babies do—like cry."

Grace wasn't usually so hostile. "Visit with your dad not good?" I'd expected nothing positive to come out of the meeting. Her dad was kind of a jerk, but generally, Grace took things in stride.

"Nope, I'd say it was a complete disaster." She put a measured scoop of powder in the bottle of water and shook. "You want me to feed him?"

"No. Come here." I patted the seat next to me, and she crawled as close as possible. In her hand was a crumpled envelope.

"Give me that critter." Mr. Chambers leaned forward with his hands held out, seeking Blue.

"You don't even like babies," Grace grumbled.

"Nonsense. It's crying babies that I don't like, and I imagine if he doesn't get his lips on the teat soon, that's exactly what he'll be."

Grace's eyes held concern. I was gathering that she'd had issues with Mr. Chambers, which didn't surprise me. The man had been a total curmudgeon when I invited him over. He relented when I added a beer to my invitation. He double-timed it when I commented on his Vietnam-veteran hat. Most of the old codgers never passed up a chance to talk military service, and he was no different.

Grace moved Blue from my arms to his. After she was sure the baby was safe, she handed him the bottle.

"It's been years since I fed a baby." He raised his bushy white brows. "For your information, young lady, I've done many a night feeding."

Grace heaved a heavy sigh. "I'm sorry, Mr. Chambers. I accused you of being a lazy dad when I didn't know you. Heck, I didn't even know you had children."

"I have three children, but they all live out of state. They converge on Fury once a year to visit their old dad and bring flowers to Darla's grave."

Grace wilted like a spent flower next to me. "I'm sorry I was so mean. I can give you a thousand excuses that range from lack of sleep to everything in between, but there is no excuse for bad behavior."

"Well …" He brushed his pudgy fingers against the drip of formula that ran down Blue's chin and wiped it on his pants. "I wasn't being neighborly either. I go to bed early because I'm old and I get up early. I wish it was different. I don't get up because the early bird gets the worm. I think I turned into the worm." He chuckled and pulled the half-empty bottle from Blue's mouth. Like a pro, he flipped the baby over and patted his back, and like me, he could pull an adult-sized burp from a tiny baby.

Grace leaned back into my side and dropped the envelope into my lap. "Blue has had allergy issues, which has made him cranky, but we've got it under control, so he won't disturb your beauty sleep anymore."

"Let's call it a truce, and instead of complaining, I'll help." He flipped the baby over again and pushed the bottle back inside Blue's mouth. I still felt bad for the kid. He had to settle for an artificial nipple when I had the real deal.

I glanced between Grace and Mr. Chambers. At least now I knew what the problem between them was, but something told me it was nothing compared to what was in that envelope.

"Can I?" I folded back the flap and waited for permission to look at her mail.

She took the envelope from my hand and pulled the paper from inside. "I need you to help me figure this out." It was a legal-looking document stating that Trenton Kehoe wanted to address paternity for Blue Faraday. "He is going to fight me for custody."

"Asshole." I tossed the page to the table and pulled her close to my side. "He has to prove Blue is his first."

"Blue is his." She said it with resignation, but I knew that DNA didn't make a daddy.

I looked at Mr. Chambers, whose frown had turned into something else. It was a look of possession. "Who's going to fight you for custody?" I'll be damned. All it took was one feeding to turn Chambers into a fan.

"Blue's father." Grace told him the story, and when she was done, the old man had a scowl that could curdle milk.

"Blue isn't going anywhere but to bed." He looked down at the sleeping baby and smiled.

Grace got up and removed Blue from the old man's lap. Once she turned the corner, Mr. Chambers spoke. "You will do right by her, right?" Suddenly he'd switched sides. He was no longer Grace's adversary. He was her advocate.

"I will do my best to protect them both." I had no idea what that would entail, but I knew what was important in life, and it wasn't the adrenaline that ran through my blood during a mission. It wasn't how fast I could clean and assemble my weapon. It was the people around me who made my heart feel so full I was certain it would burst. Grace and Blue and Ryker and Ana and Mona did that for me. Family was everything, and soon we'd find Decker so he could take his rightful place beside his brothers.

I'd lost my family years ago, but I was building a new one, one stray at a time. Something told me that Mr. Chambers was the latest addition.

He looked down at his watch. "It's *Judge Judy* time." I helped him to his unstable feet and handed him his cane. "Thanks for having me over, son." He patted me on the back, and I felt a warmth radiate through my body.

"Thanks for coming over, Mr. Chambers. Thanks for talking about your military experience, and thanks for serving your country."

The man's smile was at least sixty watts bright. "Call me Marty."

I made sure he made it down the steps and into his house before I went in search of Grace. I found her standing over Blue's crib. Silent tears dripped onto his baby blanket.

I wrapped my arms around her and kissed the top of her head. "Don't worry," I whispered, "we'll figure it out."

She swiped at the wetness on her cheeks and turned around to bury her face in my chest. "I can't lose him, Silas."

I bent over and picked her up. Her arms wrapped around my neck, and I walked her into our bedroom. *Our bedroom*, which meant that we were a team, and teams worked together for a common goal.

"I won't let that happen." I unsnapped and unzipped her jeans. "You want to talk about it first?" I tugged the material down.

She complained about her soft stomach, but I loved the feminine feel of it. She complained about her curvy hips, but I loved those too. The one thing she never complained about was my appetite for her.

"What are my options?" She gripped the edge of my T-shirt and stripped it over my head. Her fingers skated over my chest. They never failed to stop at each nick and scar-like she was mending them with her touch. What she didn't realize was she had already saved me a thousand times over. Each time her lips touched mine, she healed me.

"Ms. Faraday, it's my job to convince you that it will all work out, and I thought maybe I start with a nibble here" I nipped at her neck. "A lick here." I swept my tongue inside the curve of her ear. "A tweak here." I rolled her nipple between my thumb and finger.

A needy moan filled the air. "I'll take all the above." We removed the rest of our clothes, and I went to work on getting her to forget her morning. It only took a swipe of my tongue between her legs to set the day straight. And after an hour of Silas Savage body therapy, my Grace smiled in her sleep.

I lay next to her and thanked the universe for that one kiss on the sidewalk. Who knew that my life would change so much?

Blue made a grunt, and I rushed from the bed to get him.

"Hey, buddy. We're going to let Mommy sleep, okay?" I lifted him from the crib and took him to the changing table. Once he was clean and dry, we snuck down the hallway to the living room.

I turned on the television and turned down the volume. "What's it going to be?" I scrolled through the stations. "We have wrestling." A few channels later, I found an old John Wayne Western, but Blue didn't seem interested. It was when I got to the cartoon channel that he paid attention. I had to give it to the producers—they knew how to sell their product although it was crap. It was all in the packaging.

And that was when it hit me. The way around Trenton Kehoe was to sell him a package of crap. All I had to do was convince Grace.

Trenton Kehoe didn't want Blue. He didn't want another man to have him—classic dog pound behavior. A bone could sit in the corner of the cage untouched until another dog came sniffing around it. Grace and Blue were the bone, and I was the unwelcome dog.

Once Trenton saw how much work owning that bone would be, he'd turn around with his tail between his legs and run. The problem with him was that he'd messed with the wrong dog. I was like an angry mastiff when what I considered mine was at risk, and Grace and Blue were mine.

CHAPTER 24

GRACE

We sat in the wooden pew-like benches and waited for the judge to call our names. It reminded me of the times I'd sat in church and watched my dad help at the altar. I felt the same dread today. The judge was like the priest or the deacon. He controlled the outcome of the moment, and all I could do was sit back and take part and hope that it all turned out well for me.

Trenton had a nurse standing by to take swabs of his and Blue's cheeks. I would have thought he'd have lost interest by now. Not that he wanted Blue. He wanted to prove a point.

I knew Blue was his. Why he needed a DNA test only confirmed what Silas had said. Trenton didn't want to fight for something that wasn't a sure thing. It wasn't like he wanted to be a daddy. I believed that, like my father, Trenton was making me pay for the sins of others. He'd lost his wife because of his last affair, and I would take the punishment. He'd take away my son, so he wasn't the only one suffering.

Once the swabs were taken, a new court date was set. If Blue was his, which he was, then the next court date would be to determine custody and visitation.

We walked out of the courtroom—Silas, Blue, and I—followed by Trenton and the spit-wielding nurse.

"See you in two weeks," he said smugly.

Silas stepped forward. "About that ..." This was the moment. Silas had come up with a plan. One that he thought would work with a man like Trenton. "I'm so stoked that once the paternity comes back, you'll be able to take him half the time. That will give Grace and I some much-needed couple time."

My heart lurched in my chest. I didn't want Trenton to have a single second with Blue, let alone take him half of the time.

"I'm not your babysitter," Trenton said.

"Of course not. You're Blue's father, and I'm sure you'd expect to take him on a fifty-fifty split. Also, Grace wanted to give you his college fund information. Surely you want to match her contribution, seeing as parenting should be a partnership."

Silas kept talking while I watched Trenton's face go from a healthy pink to a flaming red.

"I'm not matching his college fund."

We walked toward the door. "I can see how that can be a burden after paying child support and medical bills."

"What are you talking about?" Trenton stopped before the exit. "I want to make sure the kid is mine. I'm not going to fight for custody."

A part of me wanted to jump for joy, and then another part of me wanted to pummel the living shit out of the man. Blue was being used as a trophy. Trenton wanted to claim him, but not take responsibility for anything.

"That's not how this works." Silas had said he'd do all the talking, but I had plenty to say. "The minute you started down this path, you opened a sinkhole. You can't claim him and not be a part of his life."

"What do you want?" He crossed his chest with his arms.

I looked at his hands and wanted to throw up. I'd let those hands roam my body. I'd allowed him the privilege of my flesh when he didn't deserve it.

"I want nothing from you. I never did. You're the one pushing this. And guess what? I will give you everything you asked for, but I will take everything Blue needs. Which means he gets half of your time, half of your resources, and all of your attention because he deserves no less than everything."

I flopped the blanket over Blue's head in preparation to go outside into the frigid air. Trenton's eyes never once went to his son. This was a game to him, and I'd showed him I knew how to play.

"We can negotiate."

"Our son isn't a business deal, Trenton. Be careful what you ask for because the courts might give it to you." I pushed through the door but still heard Silas's last words.

"Once paternity is established, we'll expect you to do your part. In fact, let's assume you'll take Blue that week. We'll bring enough to get you started. Grace can email a list of supplies you'll need from diapers to a crib. Aren't you excited?"

When I turned and looked at him, Trenton Kehoe looked anything but excited. He looked like someone who had contracted food poisoning.

Silas took the baby carrier from me, and we made our way to the SUV in silence. Once inside, I turned toward him. "Do you think he'll back down?"

"Grace, the man saw his life flash before his eyes. Everything he knows ended the minute I mentioned half. He saw bottles and diapers and a crib and a car seat and doctor's appointments and a college fund. Just one of those is enough to give the average man a rash."

"Maybe he'll be like you and warm up to the idea of a kid around." I didn't want to keep Trenton away from his son if he wanted a relationship, but I kept hearing him say *get rid of it*, like Blue was a dead rodent or trash. And he'd not once asked to hold him. Hell, the man had barely given him a glance. "I hope it doesn't come down to him taking Blue for a test drive. I'd be a basket case the minute they left."

Silas reached over the center console and held my hand. "No one's taking our baby." He said it with such strength and assurance I believed him.

"Our baby, huh?"

"A guy in my platoon named Antonio Vecchio told me that the

Italian declaration of possession is 'what's mine is mine, and what's yours is mine.' Blue is yours, therefore he's mine. Your problems are no longer yours, they're mine." He squeezed my hand before letting it go to turn the key.

"Does that mean what's yours is mine too?"

Silas nodded his head. "Every single screwed-up cell in my body belongs to you. I'm in love with you, Grace. I'm in love with Blue. You both hit me like a mortar shot to the chest."

I grabbed a tiny piece of the skin on his arm and twisted until he growled. "Hey, mister, that was romantic. Every girl wants to be compared to a device of destruction."

"Sweetheart, you're a wanton weapon. You destroyed my fantasies of an ideal life and gave me a real life—a perfect life." He pulled the car onto the four-lane street. "Where to now?"

We were in Denver, and I couldn't be in Denver without eating at Luigi's. "How about some Italian food to honor Antonio and his wise words?" I gave Silas directions to Luigi's, and I introduced him to the best lasagna he'd ever eaten.

We took a box of black and white cookies and a box of cannoli to go. There was no way I would remain Ana's friend if I didn't bring her home treats, and the last time we'd had cannoli and didn't give one to Mona, we'd heard about it for weeks. Then there was Marty, who had started joining us a couple of nights a week for dessert. I suspected he came over to hold Blue, but if he wanted to hide behind his excuse of loving my Oreo cookies, then I'd never call him on it.

Two weeks had passed, and I hadn't heard a word from Trenton, even though I'd sent him a list of baby necessities the day after our court date. Maybe our plan had backfired.

I sat in Mona's living room waiting for Silas to pick up me and Blue so we could head to Denver. He had been working on the house above the garage every day, getting it ready for the brother who may never show up.

Mona handed me a mug of steaming hot cocoa. "I put a double shot of chocolate in it. You'll need it." She sat in the black leather chair that always seemed to swallow her up and waited for me to hand her Blue.

I'd just bathed Blue, and he smelled baby powder fresh. His hair had come in. Gone was the peach fuzz, and in its place was a deep, auburn fluff.

She pulled his head to her nose. "Babies always smell so good. When do you think that stops? Because I know third graders smell like farts and boogers."

I laughed because Mona always had that effect on me. That was why Silas had insisted I come here rather than fret at home.

"What's a booger smell like?" I'd never thought of them smelling like anything.

"Not as bad as a fart." She hugged Blue to her ample chest and let out a sigh of contentment. "Not as good as this angel here."

"I'm scared, Mona. What if they give him joint custody?"

She looked up from the baby and into my eyes. "One day at a time, love. One day at a time."

CHAPTER 25

GRACE

When Silas came to pick me up, he wasn't alone. Standing behind him were Ana, Ryker, Nate, and Mr. Chambers.

I took Blue from Mona, and she said, "Let me get my coat."

"You're all coming?"

Ana put her arm around my shoulder. "You need reinforcements."

Silas put Blue in his carrier. He was good at this parenting stuff. It was like it came naturally to him. "You don't send one soldier on a mission that might require backup."

"Besides," Mr. Chambers broke in, "I want more cannoli, and I thought a big plate of spaghetti and meatballs sounded nice too."

"Let's hit it," Ryker shouted, while he shuffled Mona and Marty to his car. That would be an interesting trip since the two had no love lost for each other. Nate hopped into our back seat with Blue. A wise choice on his part.

Silas started the car, and we took off for the three-hour trip to Denver. Our appointment was the last one of the day at four o'clock.

I turned in my seat and looked at Nate. "How are things with Melissa?" It was odd to think that I had considered Nate a potential love interest. Looking at him now, I knew he was wrong for me. All wrong.

"Over," he said with no emotion. "She traded me in for a frat boy."

"The girl has no idea what she's missing." I knew Nate to be a sweetheart and loyal friend. He wasn't the peacock kind of man I used to like, but he also wasn't the badass I'd grown to love. "I used to think I liked one kind of man, and then I met this one." I tapped Silas on the shoulder, and he smiled. "I think the right one will come along when you least expect it."

"Oh, I'm already dating her. Sabrina might not be the right one, but she's the right one for now." Apparently, Nate was giving man-whore Mondays a new twist. The thought made me smile, if only briefly.

We arrived at the courthouse with a few minutes to spare, and when we stepped inside the building, my stomach twisted into a braid. Standing in the entry of the courthouse was my father, and he was talking to Trenton.

I wanted to turn and run, or maybe rush forward and punch both of them in the nose, but I did neither. This was my life, and I had to own it. I stood my ground and watched as my father approached us.

"Grace." He nodded and then looked at Silas. "Good to see you, Silas." He dropped to his haunches and pulled away the light blanket that covered Blue. "Hey there, Blue." He tickled the baby's cheek with the pad of his pointer finger.

It took everything inside of me to not push him away. "What are you doing here?"

"Trenton told me about the meeting. I had something to say to him." He stood and looked at me with tired green eyes. I wasn't sure whether I saw compassion or regret looking back at me, but there was something besides his usual disdain. "When are you going to baptize my grandson?" Of course, Dad would slide into church mode. It was what he always did when he wanted to hide.

"I've been busy, Dad, with this whole shit storm that you stirred up. I plan to get to it." Ryker and Ana entered the courthouse with Mona and Marty in tow. I looked at my best friend and her man. "I've got his godparents chosen."

Dad nodded and said, "Trenton is doing the right thing."

I let out an exasperated breath. "How do you know?" I didn't think it was the right thing at all. How could a man who couldn't bother to answer an email be responsible for a human being?

"Because I told him what he needed to do."

I couldn't stand there another minute. "I've got to go, Dad. My fate awaits me in that room."

He reached up and touched my cheek. "Grace, have a little faith, okay?"

Faith was all I had left. And then I turned around and saw my supporters. Everyone needed a village, and I'd brought mine from Fury.

Things were different this time in court. We stood in front of the judge. I thought it would be Trenton, Blue, and me, but he'd brought a lawyer—and that made my head spin. Did I need a lawyer?

The gang sat in a row of chairs that lined the back wall. I looked toward Silas because his presence gave me strength. Ana held Ryker's arm while Mona leaned forward, trying to focus on something. Marty tapped his cane against the floor until Nate fisted the handle and made him stop.

The judge held the envelope in his hand. "I have the results. Are you ready?"

He looked at me first. I nodded. Then he looked at Trenton, who looked at his lawyer.

"Your Honor? My client has changed his mind. He's willing to sign over all rights to Blue Faraday right now if Ms. Faraday agrees to not demand anything from my client."

I let out a gasp, and the tears flowed. Silas was right. The first sign of anything that might require time or money or a heart had sent Trenton running for cover.

The judge slammed his hands down on his desk like a gavel. "Why are you wasting my time, Mr. Kehoe? Do you think it's funny to burden the courts with your games?"

"No, sir."

"Why the change of heart?" The judge opened the envelope and looked at the results. "You're willing to give up your son?" There was no mistaking his intent; his phrasing confirmed that Blue was, in fact, Trenton Kehoe's flesh and blood.

"I've spent a lot of the last two weeks soul searching. I even consulted a spiritual advisor who informed me DNA didn't make a daddy." He looked at me with an apologetic expression. "I never wanted Blue, and I have no right to ask for him. He's just another accomplishment—a trophy on my shelf. He doesn't belong there. He belongs with his mother." Trenton turned to my supporters, who were now all on their feet. "He belongs to her family."

It took fifteen minutes for us to complete the paperwork and another thirty for me to stop crying.

It was Mona who got us moving. "I need cannoli before I die. I'm old, and that could be any second."

Not wanting to be the reason for Mona's death, we left the courthouse triumphant and hungry.

At Luigi's we ordered family style and had a feast. At the table were all my favorite people. We passed Blue around until he'd made it through everyone twice. The day wore him out too, and soon he was in his carrier and fast asleep.

I watched the people around me. It was the only thing Trenton had gotten right on his own: They were my family. And that made me think of my father, who for the first time in my life had stood up and done the right thing. I snapped a picture of Blue sleeping and sent it to him with the message, *Your grandson thanks you.*

A few minutes later, I got a reply: *Your mother and I would like to visit soon.*

Mom knows? I texted back. I still hadn't told her about Blue. I wasn't sure how she'd take it. She'd never been a doting mother, and I didn't think she would be an interested grandmother.

Yes, and she can't wait to meet her grandson.

Turns out I was wrong. I'd been wrong about a lot of things, but there was one thing I was right about, and that was Silas. None of this would have been possible without him.

After a few more texts and a plan for a visit soon, I put away my phone and enjoyed the company and the food and the calm.

Marty lifted a forkful of spaghetti to Mona's mouth, and she took it.

"Watch out, Mona, he might have something contagious," Ryker teased.

Mona blushed and waved him off with a dismissive hand. When she finished chewing she said, "Oh, pish, the only thing Marty has that I can catch is a bad attitude."

"Now, Mona, be nice or I'll have to turn you over my knee."

The rest of us stared at the old couple. That comment had put us on full tilt. "Are you getting sweet on him?" I asked my favorite septuagenarian.

"Honey, you can't sweeten vinegar. Besides, I'm too old for that kind of stuff."

Old my ass. I'd heard her go full-on cougar with Silas and Ryker. "I don't believe you for a minute, Mona."

"Smart girl," Marty said before he forked a piece of meatball into her mouth. He was working his way into Mona's heart one bite at a time.

We were all too stuffed to order dessert, so we took home five to-go boxes stuffed with pizzelles, cannoli, and black and white cookies.

When we reached Fury, everyone went their own way. They were all tired from a stressful day, but my Silas was ready to celebrate.

He opened a bottle of wine and had two glasses poured and on the coffee table when I came out from putting Blue to bed.

I looked around the house I'd once hated. It no longer felt cold on winter nights because Silas was there to warm it up.

We sat next to each other with our glasses raised for a toast. "Here's to family," he said. "Here's to Ryker being a father. Here's to me being a father. Here's to you for loving me. I don't deserve you, Grace, but I will not argue about keeping you. You're mine."

I loved it when he got possessive of Blue and me. Silas was nicknamed Rooster, but he could never be confused with a listless bird that pecked at everything around him. In fact, if I hadn't known better, I would have categorized him as a bird of prey like his brother, Hawk. He dove in and went after what he wanted. How lucky for me to be his prey. Proves that the true character of a man has nothing to do with the feathers he fluffs and shows off, but everything to do with the heart they cover.

CHAPTER 26

SILAS

Grace paced the hardwood floor, waiting for her mom and dad to arrive. She had changed her clothes twice and checked her makeup at least a dozen times. Even Blue was in his third outfit. And his tufts of auburn hair were slicked back with baby oil.

I'd thrown on a pair of jeans and was deemed perfect, but then again, Grace always thought I was perfect. The woman wore blinders when she looked at me.

I walked over to the window where her head went from side to side looking for her father's white sedan to appear. "It will be fine." I cradled Blue in my arms. "If it isn't, I'll drop-kick them to the curb."

"You'd do that for me?" She leaned into my body, and I gave her a reassuring smile.

"Sweetheart, there are few people I'd do anything for, but you and Blue and Ryker and Ana are tops on my list."

"I'm so in love with you." She rose on her toes and gave me a chaste kiss. Anything more intimate and she knew I'd have her in the bedroom flat on her back regardless of who was arriving.

"I love you too. So much it scares me." Since that day in the courthouse a week ago, when there was the real possibility of losing Blue part time, I'd continued to live my life as if my time could run out at any minute. It was the reason I had a clock tattooed on my chest. But I'd had it wrong back then. I'd lived carelessly. I lived on the dangerous periphery. If I were smack dab in the center of things, it was not for the good. It meant that I was taunting the universe to take me. That was changing. I wanted to live smack dab in the center of Grace's love. I wanted my time to tick by with minutes of family and friends surrounding me. I wanted to make sure I didn't miss an opportunity to show the people who mattered how much I loved them.

I didn't have parents, not in the real sense, so this was as exciting for me. I'd had a decent set of foster parents at the end. They loved their kids, and they seemed taken with me, but by that point, my heart had hardened, and my ability to trust was all but gone.

It would be interesting to watch the family dynamic between Grace and her estranged parents.

Her body stiffened, and I knew they were here. A white Lexus pulled into our driveway, and Will Faraday rushed to the other side of the car to help his wife, Jill, out. Will and Jill … I couldn't make this shit up if I tried.

Grace's mom was lovely, an older version of her daughter. My heart pumped rapidly with the knowledge that if I were lucky enough, I'd be able to watch Grace grow into a better version of the woman coming up the walkway.

"You got this." I kissed her on the cheek and gave her a nudge toward the door.

"I haven't seen her in over a year." Her voice quaked like maybe she would cry, but the look in her eyes told me as long as I stayed close, she'd be fine.

"I'm not going anywhere, Grace."

She let out a breath, and the tension visibly eased from her shoulders.

We walked to the door where, through the poorly insulated door, we heard her mother tell her father how nervous she was. A small smile appeared on Grace's face.

"She's nervous too," she whispered, knowing voices carried through the walls.

Grace opened the door before her parents knocked, and as soon as her mother saw her, she burst into tears.

"Oh, Grace, I'm so sorry."

Will stepped around his wife and came to stand next to me while the two women fell into each other's arms and wept.

There were words of sorrow and pleas for forgiveness, and after at least a dozen hugs, Jill stepped into the house and zoned in on me.

"Who's this handsome guy?" I was sure she was talking about Blue, who was wide awake and enjoying the stimulation of new guests, but when she walked up and cupped my cheek, I realized she was talking about me.

I hefted Blue, who was now over ten pounds, into one arm and held out my hand to Grace's mother. "I'm Silas."

"Will has wonderful things to say about you, Silas." I wasn't certain if I was shocked or not. Will Faraday was a waffler these days. He couldn't seem to make up his mind about much, but I saw a trend happening. He was seeing life differently too. Maybe he needed a big clock etched into his chest to help him remember that time was fleeting.

Jill's eyes went from my face down to Blue, who couldn't control his limbs.

"Would you like to hold him?" I held the baby out, but she didn't take him.

"Mom, you can hold him," Grace said. "You raised me, and I turned out okay." Grace pulled Blue from my arms and walked him over toward the couch where she sat. When her mother sat beside her, Grace put the baby in her arms, and the woman practically melted into the fabric of the cushions. Blue had that effect on everyone. He turned the hardest person into emotional goo.

"Coffee or tea, anyone?" I asked.

Three requests for coffee came immediately. Even Blue made a grunt, but he'd have to settle for formula.

"I'll help," Will said and followed me into the kitchen.

"Looks like you and Mrs. Faraday are mending fences." I set four K-Cups on the counter and pulled out the milk and sugar.

"We are. She's even considering moving back to Denver." Will pulled four cups from the cupboard while I waited for the machine to preheat. "What about you, son? Are you going to make an honest woman out of my Grace?"

Laughter burst from inside me. "Grace doesn't need me to make her honest. She's brutally honest on her own."

"You know what I mean, Silas." His tone went serious.

I knew what he meant, but I wasn't taking the bait. "Grace and I are fine the way we are right now. I don't need a marriage certificate to prove she loves me. She doesn't need one to keep me around. You of all people should understand that a piece of paper doesn't make a marriage." I set a cup aside and let Will doctor it up for his wife.

He added a single teaspoon of sugar and a splash of cream before he said anything. "I'm still old-fashioned that way, but I'm learning. There is a huge disconnect between what I know in my heart and what the world wants to see."

"Go with your heart. It seems to lead you in a better direction." I had to give the man credit. He'd turned the custody thing around so Grace never had to worry about it again. Or maybe we'd scared the living hell out of Trenton with our talk of college funds and the cost of diapers. Grace and I agreed that we'd be honest with Blue about his father, and if either of them ever wanted to meet the other, we'd set it up.

Once the coffees were made, we brought them into the living room where Jill and Grace were sharing baby stories. It brought me back to a time when Decker was a baby and we all sat around him and stared. To a six-year-old, it was like science fiction. One day the baby was in your mom's tummy, and the next, it was on a blanket in the living room.

I didn't understand how kids were created back then, but I was a huge fan of the process now. Although Grace and I were careful to not make another kid too soon, I was excited about the prospect of Grace's belly big with my child.

Blue got cranky, and I could smell the reason. "I'll get it." I lifted the baby from his grandmother's lap.

"He changes diapers too?" Jill looked at me like a halo glowed above my head, and then she scowled at her husband. "Will, look at that. He's an active participant."

Will shook his head. "The boy is smarter than I ever was."

I started toward Blue's bedroom. "I'd helped out a lot with my baby brother, Decker. Even at six years old, I had diapers down to an art." I nodded toward the baby's room, and Will followed me. He had a lot of diaper changes to make up for.

We came out five minutes later with Will looking like he'd survived the Battle of the Bulge or some other big war, but there was a look of accomplishment on his face once you got past his upturned nose.

"When are the others coming?" Will asked. He was itching to get Blue baptized. You could take the man out of the church, but there was no taking the church out of the man. Since Grace wasn't a huge fan of organized religion, she didn't want the big church ordeal. Anyone could baptize a person. All it took were willing participants and water.

Those participants showed up an hour later. Ana came with Ryker, and Mona snuck out of Marty's house and up to the door. Because she was nearly blind, she didn't realize that we could all see her adjust her dress and smooth down her hair. And if I wasn't mistaken, Marty's lips had taken on the orange hue of Mona's lipstick.

Inside the tiny living room, Will baptized Blue. Despite Grace's misgivings about her father, she knew the baptism was important to him. It was a turning point in their relationship where Grace could appreciate her father's gifts and he could appreciate Grace.

Blue, on the other hand, wasn't a fan of the holy water, and it took his grandmother's bosom and a full bottle of formula to calm him down.

CHAPTER 27

GRACE

Was this really my life? Did Silas slide into bed beside me each night and hold me in his arms? Did he fight me for the middle-of-the-night feedings?

I'd asked for a lot in my life. I wanted fame and fortune and a twenty-four-inch waist. I got so much more.

"Are you ready, Blue?" At three months old, he was growing up way faster than I liked. I hefted his carrier up and snapped him into the car. "Daddy's waiting for us."

The first time Silas had said, "Come to Daddy," I'd burst into tears. There was a time when I'd thought my son would never hear those words, but he heard them every day along with *Daddy's boy, Daddy's little buddy, Daddy loves you.* Silas had been an amazing father to Blue and an amazing man for me.

Tonight was fried chicken night. It was the one thing Ana craved with regularity along with chocolate cake, so every Wednesday night we met her and Ryker at the diner to have a family dinner.

Silas and Ryker were almost finished with the house above the garage. They worked mornings in the shop with Ryker repairing bikes and Silas repairing the mess Ryker had made of the books. The afternoons were spent with paint and plaster.

We'd all truly settled into our lives, and it was impossible to imagine being any happier. Even Blue seemed to know how lucky we were, based on his excited coo when I said, "Let's go pick up Auntie Ana."

When I pulled up in front of Ana's house, she waddled out to the car. At seven months along, she was in full bloom, and pregnancy looked good on her.

"I'm starved." She climbed into the front seat and tugged on the safety belt to gain space for her belly.

"You're always starved." I put the car in reverse and headed toward the best things in life … chocolate cake … fried chicken … Savage men.

"Aren't you the woman who could eat a box of black and white cookies at one sitting?"

I held my hand in the air and waved. "That's me, and I hold the record. Are you going to challenge it?"

She pulled at the knit shirt that hugged her tummy. "I'll stick with the cake."

A few minutes later, we arrived at the diner, but it wasn't the calm place it normally was. Outside a crowd gathered around a man who lay prone and still on the sidewalk. Silas and Ryker stood over him. Hannah sat collapsed against the building in tears.

Ana practically flew from the car, and as soon as I could park and get Blue out of his seat, I did the same. Ryker had moved and was already holding Ana. His words broke my heart. "I'm so sorry, baby. I couldn't let him beat her and get away with it." Tears ran down his face. He kneeled before her and kissed her belly like he was saying goodbye. "I'm so sorry."

Silas turned in my direction, his expression conflicted as he looked from me to Blue and then to his brother. The man next to him groaned. In the distance, the sound of a siren echoed through the air.

Everything was in his expression. Rage and sorrow warred within him. "This is bullshit." He picked the guy up by the collar and told him to open his eyes. "Look at me, asshole. I don't want there to be any doubt about who beat the shit out of you." He shook the guy, and when the man opened his eyes, he punched him in the face and let him drop back to the asphalt.

Silas pulled me off to the side of the crowd. "Grace, I'm so sorry. I can't let him go to jail again. He went to jail for me once. I have to go for him this time." Silas looked over at his brother, who was still on his knees in front of Ana.

I stood there, stunned into silence. This was supposed to be fried chicken and chocolate cake night. Those were happy things; this, whatever it was, was not.

Silas told me to stay put and walked over to his brother. "You need to leave, bro." He pulled his brother to a standing position and pushed him toward the Subaru. "Go now. You've got Ana and a kid to take care of. You did this for me once. Let me do it for you now."

"You're not taking the fall for my actions." Ryker pushed against his brother, and I thought they'd throw fists at each other. "He saw me. He knows I hit him." Ryker looked toward Hannah, who still sat against the wall with her hands buried in her face.

I was torn. I wanted to pull Silas to me and tell him he couldn't give up everything we had, and then I looked at Ana, whose hands were wrapped around her pregnant belly. Her eyes focused on the man she loved, the man who had already paid for a thousand sins he never committed, and I knew there was no choice.

I rushed to my friend and told her to take Ryker home. If they weren't at the scene, they couldn't be questioned. I stared at all the witnesses, and I wondered whether they would confirm the lie I knew Silas would tell.

Ryker and Ana didn't budge, and something in me knew they wouldn't. Ryker was the type of man to take responsibility for what he did. He'd proved that over the past twenty years. And Ana would never let another person take the fall.

The blame for the Fury massacre had sat on Ryker's shoulders until Ana thought she'd been the one to cause it all. Then they both learned the truth. It wasn't either of them, but a Rebel named Tiny who started it all. There was no way my friend was letting Silas take the rap. Pregnant or not, Ana couldn't live with the guilt.

Silas walked to Hannah and moved her hands from her face. There was a red hand mark on her right cheek. I kneeled beside her with Blue in my arms.

"What happened?" Someone had to make sense of all this mess, and since Hannah seemed to be in the middle of it, I hoped she could shed light on why Ryker was waiting to go back to prison and why Silas was volunteering to take his place.

Hannah sucked in a few ragged breaths. "He followed me." She hiccupped and swiped at her swollen eyes. "I parked, and he attacked me."

"Who is he?" I looked at the man who was now in a sitting position. Someone had handed him a wad of napkins from the diner to hold against his bloody nose.

"Cameron Longfellow." She looked at the man and then cried again.

That name sounded familiar, but I couldn't place his face. Then again, one of his eyes was nearly swollen shut, and his nose now curved off to the side.

Sheriff Stuart pulled into the parking lot with sirens blaring. The sound wound down as he exited the car and walked to where the crowd stood.

He assessed the situation and stepped into the middle of the crowd. "Can someone tell me what's going on here?" He scanned the parking lot, looking for the one person who would spill the beans, but it didn't appear that anyone was talking.

Word traveled fast in a small town, and within minutes even Marty and Mona were here, checking out the big event at the diner.

"You need an ambulance?" the sheriff asked Cameron.

The man shook his head and tried to stand, but he was wobbly on his feet and fell back to his butt. "I want to press charges." His voice was nasal, and his nose made the kind of whistling sound that happened when you were stuffed up.

Sheriff Stuart looked around the crowd. "Who hit you, and why would they do that?"

Hannah scrambled to her feet. She raced to the sheriff. "He

attacked me." She dropped her head and, in a muffled voice, said, "I fought back and he hit me." Her hand reached for her blazing red cheek.

The sheriff looked at Cameron. "You did this to him." He chuckled and then adopted his stern sheriff demeanor.

"I ignored his advances, but he pushed for what he wanted." She looked around at the people staring at her. "I thought he would rape me."

Those words tore at my gut. No woman deserved that treatment, and I was proud of Silas and Ryker for coming to her rescue. Few men would have.

"You want to press charges?" Sheriff Stuart gave her a look that said *please say yes*, but Hannah shook her head no, and there was an audible gasp from the crowd.

"He's the Pine Creek mayor's son. He'll get a slap on the wrist while I get much worse. Nothing sticks to slime like that."

Cameron let out a chuckle that made me want to punch him in the nose. "Damn it, Sheriff. I want to press charges. I'm the victim here."

"It's your right," the sheriff said, "but remember, there are a lot of witnesses. Now tell me: Who hit you?"

Something strange came over me in that instant. Maybe it was the fact I loved Silas more than I loved myself. Maybe I thought the Savage men had paid their debt to society, or maybe I knew the sheriff wouldn't send me to jail.

I stepped forward and said, "I hit him."

Both Ryker and Silas snapped their heads in my direction, but a funny thing happened. Other people stepped forward to claim the assault.

Ana was first. "I hit him." She clenched her fists at her sides.

Marty followed. He shuffled forward with his cane in hand and said, "I did it. I hit that bastard."

Mona stood in front of the sheriff, only she wasn't looking at him when she confessed. Lord knows she couldn't see him. She stared off into the distance, fisted up, and swung at nothing. "I hit him. A clean right hook is all it took to make him crumble."

She turned toward Marty, and I swear she mumbled the words *weak bastard* but when the sheriff asked her to repeat what she'd said, she replied, "Next week's a bastard, Sheriff." She lifted her right Clarks loafer. "Corn removal."

One by one, the townsfolk took turns until the sheriff had eighteen names on his list.

Cameron Longfellow looked straight at Ryker and Silas and said, "They hit me, and I want them in jail."

In spite of the mass confessions, Sheriff Stuart couldn't overlook that accusation, and Ryker and Silas couldn't deny their involvement. They were the type of men who owned their shit.

He didn't handcuff them. In fact, he went into the diner and bought them a meal to go before he told them to climb into the back of his squad car.

"You two need to call a lawyer," he said to Ana and me. "These are bullshit charges, but I know Mayor Longfellow, and he has friends in high places even though his son is a bottom feeder." He walked us over to his car where he told us to give our men a kiss goodbye.

"We'll be down to bail you out in a few minutes," I said to Silas.

Cameron Longfellow yelled from a distance, "See you in court, assholes." He looked at Hannah, who was icing her cheek. "I'll see you soon, sweetheart." Then he cackled like a crazy person, climbed into his Porsche SUV, and took off.

"Call Henry and ask him to look into Cameron," Ryker said before Sheriff Stuart closed the doors and drove away.

Ana and I knew Sheriff Stuart wouldn't mistreat our men. Ever since that day in front of his house when the truth came out, they had forged a friendship. Sheriff Stuart had stopped being Junior or Sheriff and had become Sam. He was no different from any of the other boys of Fury. He was a victim of a tragic event and a survivor, and he'd become a friend.

CHAPTER 28

SILAS

Sitting in the sheriff's office sucked, but it could have been worse. Sam didn't lock us up in a cell. He took our statements while we ate the fried chicken and waffles he'd ordered for us, then he sent us home.

"What did he say?" Grace asked as soon as we got back to her place. She hurried around the house straightening up. Grace was a neat freak already, but add in some stress, and the feather duster and damp mop always appeared.

I pulled Blue from his carrier and held him close to my chest. I'd found my happy place, and I would lose it. I kissed his head a dozen times, knowing I'd never be able to give him enough kisses before I would have to leave him.

"He said to get a lawyer." I sat on the overstuffed red chair and cradled the baby in my arms while Grace moved everything from the bookshelves and removed the invisible dust.

"Okay, we'll get a lawyer." She looked around for something else to clean.

"Grace." I moved to the cream-colored sofa and patted the space beside me. "Come sit down."

She looked at the duster and then at me and tossed the duster to the floor in the corner. She sat next to me and burst out in tears. "Silas, I can't lose you." She buried her head in my shoulder and put a hand on Blue's leg.

It hadn't taken long for us to become a family. We were connected in ways I still hadn't figured out. I gazed at this redheaded spitfire who stole my breath, and then I looked down at Blue, the baby who'd stolen my heart.

Months ago, I couldn't imagine a life shared with anyone, and today I couldn't imagine my life without them.

"This will not go well for Ryker and me." I cradled Blue in one arm and wrapped the other around Grace, who was trying to get her tears under control.

Acid churned in my stomach and threatened to burn a hole through me. Finally, I had two good things—four if you counted my brother and Ana, five if you added Mona—and I would lose them all.

Jail didn't sound appealing no matter how you cut it. I'd stepped in to take the fall so Ryker wouldn't end up there again, and now we'd both be going to jail. We had two strikes against us. First, we were Savages. That alone came with a reputation that hadn't died when our father did. Second, Cameron Longfellow's father was the mayor, and you didn't get in a position like that without a lot of support from people in high places. Guilty or not, we were going down.

Grace covered Blue's ears and then whispered, "It's bullshit."

"I agree, but it is what it is, and we'll figure it out."

"If Hannah would have stepped forward ..." Grace growled. "I like her, but I hate her."

"You can't blame her. She's right. It's her word against his, and with his connections, his word will carry more weight. She'd come out of court broke and beaten down." Deep inside I wished that Hannah had stepped up too, but I understood. People like us didn't get the benefit of the doubt.

Later that night I made love to Grace. We spent hours wrapped in each other's arms. I wasn't sure how many nights I had left in those arms. All I knew was that I wanted every minute I could get.

A week later, we were in court for the first time. We stood in front of Judge Davis while he looked over the facts of the case.

On paper, it looked like two thugs from Fury, Colorado, beat the pulp out of an upstanding citizen. This was a preliminary meeting to decide whether we wanted a jury of our peers or the judge to decide.

Given that our family name preceded us and the name Savage rarely added up to a vision of model citizenship, Ryker and I opted to have the judge hear the case and deliver the sentence. One peer didn't seem as frightening as a group of peers.

The gavel hit the desk with a thud that sounded so final, and I wondered if it was a sign. Would he drop that gavel as hard when he decided our fates?

"Given the charges—" He looked at Ryker. "—and the prior conviction for violence from one defendant, I will hear the case." He flipped his calendar to the next month and set up the hearing.

Our lawyer said nothing. We weren't paying him much, and his silence proved he wasn't offering us much for our money.

The judge looked at Ryker and me. We'd dressed up for the day. Both of us were in slacks, a button-down shirt, and a tie. Requirements from Ana and Grace. We knew it wouldn't sway the court, but it made the girls feel better, so we'd done it.

"Court date set for four weeks from today." The gavel struck the wood desk with another boom, and we filed out of the small courthouse to a sunny day. I had four more weeks of sun and sweet Grace.

CHAPTER 29

GRACE

Silas held me like he might lose me, and deep down inside we both knew it was a possibility. We maintained our normal routine of having breakfast together before he went off to work at the garage. He always kissed me long and soft before he climbed into Ryker's Subaru and drove away.

It was a shame how everything had taken a turn toward shit as business had picked up and they were making a livable income. What would happen if they went to jail? Business would die, and another dream would be lost. Hadn't the Savages paid enough? People talked about karma, and I spent a lot of time wondering when the good shit would make its way to Ryker and Silas. Lately, karma was a disgruntled, damn twat-waffle of a bitch whose tally of good deeds was skewed.

Ana and I would keep up with the taxes and upkeep of the property, but once again The Nest would be empty.

It was French Toast Friday, and I sat in front of Ana's house waiting for her to join Blue and me. Ryker didn't like her driving, so I'd become her personal chauffeur, which gave me something to do.

"Sorry," she apologized after she opened the door. "I had a file to send to a client." She pressed her bottom into the seat first and swung her legs and stomach inside. It didn't help that I had an SUV that sat off the ground.

Watching Ana work her way through pregnancy was comical. Between the cravings and the complaints, she was never boring. I was sure I had offered her comic relief regularly with all my fears and foibles.

"It's no problem. Blue and I grew our hair out and noted a new wrinkle while we waited."

Ana reached over and swatted my arm. "I wasn't that late."

"Are you ready to go put pressure on Hannah?" I backed out of the driveway and headed for the diner.

"I'm not her biggest fan because she was so awful to me. Do you remember when she told me I was a fad?"

"Yeah, and so much for that—Ryker's child was already growing inside you." I drove through the streets of Fury and smiled. This town had grown on me. "I don't know if I should be angry with her or feel sorry for her. She's got a story. Who hangs out in a town like Fury?"

Ana turned toward me and gave me a look that said, *'really?'* "We live in Fury."

"I know, but it's not a town for young single women who aren't homeless or pregnant. I get us, but Hannah is pretty, and she's smart."

"Have you ever asked about her story? We all have one."

I hated it when Ana went all armchair psychologist on me. She was as bad as Mona, only Mona made me laugh, whereas Ana made me think. "No, I've never asked."

We arrived at the diner in time for the breakfast rush, which meant over five people were in the place at one time. We took up what was now deemed our booth and waited for Hannah to bring us coffee. Gone were the days where I had to chase her down. Now, without prompting, she brought decaf for Ana and regular for me.

She poured two-handed and filled us up at the same time. "You doing okay?" I asked. Her bruised face had gone from red to purple and was now taking on the color of moldy cheese with its green and yellow streaks.

She shrugged. "I'm hanging in there." She didn't offer much more before she walked away.

"Grace, don't say anything to her, okay?" Ana put several packets of sugar into her coffee and stirred.

"Our men will go to jail because they defended her. The least she can do is step up and do her part." I was so tempted to get up and drag the blonde back to the booth and hold her hostage until she agreed to press charges, but the bell above the door rang and Marty and Mona walked in. They slid in our booth uninvited.

"French Toast Friday," Mona said and clapped her hands like a kindergartener.

I stared at Ana. "Are you sure you aren't related?"

Mona gave me a hard look. "What's got your knickers in a twist?"

I turned toward her on the bench next to me. Marty took the seat next to Ana. "What's wrong?" I gulped my coffee like it was a stiff shot of whiskey. "That girl can file charges, which will prove that Ryker's and Silas's actions were justified. It may not get them off completely, but at least it will cast doubt on Cameron Cocksucker Longfellow, who probably has a tiny penis, and that's why he has to stalk women and beat on them."

Marty and Mona stared at me. The whole table went mute. "Do you know her story?" Mona finally asked after seconds of nothing.

My eyes snapped to Ana. "You know something I don't?"

Ana shook her head. "I know nothing. I heard rumors. That's all." Ana looked to Mona and Marty. "Do you two know her story?"

Mona shook her head, but Marty spoke. "She has a tough life. She takes care of her mother, who's a shell of a woman since her overdose."

"It wasn't the overdose that cracked her mom's shell, it was that no-good boyfriend of hers who went after Hannah a few years ago." Mona looked around as if she could see her surroundings, and then she leaned into the center of the table and whispered. "Hannah's mom shot him. If you ask me, she should have killed him, but she didn't shoot to kill, she shot to stop him. They went to court, and the mom was charged with reckless endangerment of a child."

My hand covered my mouth. "Did she refuse to testify then too?" It wouldn't have surprised me.

Marty let out a sigh. "She testified, and they didn't believe her. His word against hers."

The bright lights of the diner dimmed, and my stomach coiled into knots. "Poor Hannah." I hadn't considered her reasons for not coming forward. I'd been selfish and thought only about what I wanted: Silas.

Hannah skipped over and pulled her order pad from her pocket. "French toast for everyone?"

We nodded, and she left. I sat there for minutes, thinking about how I'd judged her without knowing her. Wasn't that what my father had done with me? What a town had done to Ryker? What Ryker had done to Ana? Life was a vicious damn circle.

Ana broke the silence. "So, Marty, I saw you sneaking out of Mona's house early this morning." Ana narrowed her eyes at him. She had taken to not wearing contacts, and her one blue and one brown eye were striking. "What are your intentions toward my girl here?"

Mona gave her a dismissive wave. "Oh, pish. You want to talk about his intentions when both of you are shacking up with your hotties?"

Marty reached across the table and placed his age-spotted hand over Mona's. "She uses me for sex." They both couldn't control their laughter. In fact, they laughed so hard the other four people in the diner couldn't look away.

"I got you a new tie." I held up the conservative blue tie I bought for Silas to wear to court tomorrow.

"You think it will work?" Silas approached me and took the silky fabric from my hands.

"It's worth a try." We knew a tie couldn't sway an opinion, but it wouldn't hurt to show up to court looking like an accountant. People respected ties and suits and penny loafers.

"It is worth a try." He walked me back to the edge of the bed and covered my eyes with the tie. "Lay back, sweetheart, and I will leave you with a night to remember."

"You're not leaving me, Silas."

He fastened the fabric around my head and guided me to my back. First to go were my shoes. My pants, and shirt, and undergarments followed them until I lay bare in front of him with only his new tie.

"Listen to me, Grace." Fabric swished and fell to the floor. "I may have to leave you. Not by choice, sweetheart." His naked body climbed up mine.

I fisted my hands because that was a lie. I knew he'd had his reasons, but he had also had a choice. "You chose, Silas. You defended your brother." I reached to uncover my eyes, and he stopped me.

His calloused fingers traced up my stomach until he reached my heart. "I made the only choice I could. I owed my brother, and now, for better or for worse, the debt is paid." The bed dipped, and his lips kissed that space on my collarbone. The place that always sent shivers down my spine. "I don't want to leave you, Grace. I love you."

"I love you too, Silas. I can't survive without you." A lump of raw emotion overwhelmed me, but I refused to cry. Silas didn't need my tears. He needed my strength.

"You will survive. You were doing okay before I came along. You'll do okay if I have to leave." His breath heated my lips. His body pressed against mine. He probed at my entrance.

"I pray they don't take you away." My voice quaked. I swallowed the dry-toast-like sorrow stuck in my throat.

"Grace, I want you to live and to love." His body shifted, and something wet hit my face. The blindfold wasn't put on me to give me a night to remember; it was to save me from a vision I'd never forget—Silas was crying silent tears.

"I love you, Silas. There will be no other. I'll wait. Blue will wait." I gripped his hips and pulled him deep inside of me. "You're worth the wait."

CHAPTER 30

SILAS

Grace and Blue sat on the bench behind me. I couldn't believe it had been a month since Cameron's beating. Both Ryker and I regretted not hitting him harder. Maybe he would have lost his memory if I'd used my right fist instead of my left, but I didn't want to kill the asshole, teach him a lesson: that you didn't abuse women.

The mayor had pressed for second-degree assault and battery charges and vowed to get us a lengthy sentence. However, they'd lowered the charges to third-degree assault and battery. The charges were still bullshit, but at least that allowed Ryker and me to live at home while we awaited trial. It also gave Ryker the time he needed to get Ana set up for the birth of their child and the possibility that he'd be serving time.

I'd spent the past thirty days falling more in love with Grace and Blue. What was there not to love? She was funny and sexy, and she was mine. And Blue was everything a man could hope for in a son. With Grace's guidance, he'd grow into a fine man.

Henry had been in the background trying to dig up dirt on Cameron, but nothing had panned out yet.

Ana and Grace had given up putting pressure on Hannah to press charges. I understood her reluctance. A man like Cameron would get away with near murder because he would be judged by who his father was, not by the shitty things he'd done. Hannah, on the other hand, would simply be judged.

Ryker and I had found a new lawyer, one who had a voice. A man named Thomas Lowell, who was a friend of Sam Stuart. You knew you were in good hands when the sheriff arranged for your legal counsel.

We sat in silence and waited for our lives to change again.

The judge walked out of his chambers dressed in black robes and took his place at the high desk in front of the tiny courtroom. Fury didn't have its own judge, so several surrounding towns shared the magistrate. That didn't bode well for Ryker and I since Judge Davis also represented the town of Pine Creek.

Ryker looked over his shoulder to Ana, who sat behind him with her hands splayed on her belly.

"I love you, baby," he said in a voice that would have gotten him labeled as a pussy-whipped bastard if we weren't sitting here looking at real time.

"I love you too, Hawk." She blew him a kiss. That woman was a keeper, and I was damn proud of my brother for having won her heart.

No one knew the sex of the baby. They refused to find out in advance. Even in the midst of Ryker potentially serving time, they held to their decision.

Ana was about four weeks from delivery, and I never missed a chance to let my brother know how disappointed I was that he hadn't let me take responsibility, but he always reminded me that I had a family too.

I looked over my shoulder at Grace and smiled. Here I was sitting in court with a possible sentence of two years, and I still considered myself the luckiest bastard in the world because Grace loved me. She loved me enough to share her son—our son.

The judge hit the gavel on the desk and said, "Let's begin."

Cameron sat with his pricey suit, his pricey lawyer, and his big-shot dad, and smirked.

The judge went through the charges, and honestly, none of them were trumped up. Ryker beat the man to a pulp, and I finished the job. Not only had we been charged with third-degree assault and battery, but Cameron was also suing us for collateral damages. Those items were bullshit too because I was certain he didn't need plastic surgery for his nose or a full set of veneers for the chip in his tooth. It didn't matter, though, because Ryker and I would do the time and pay the fine. We knew how this worked. Ryker had a rap sheet, and I was guilty by association.

"You ready for this, bro?" I slapped him on the back and turned toward the judge who rambled on about fair sentencing and a bunch of other crap. He said something about pillars of the community, but he wasn't looking at us. He was staring at the mayor and his asinine son. When he mentioned taming the riffraff, he stared directly at us.

"Maybe we'll be cellmates," Ryker joked. We couldn't do much more than laugh at a bad situation. If we didn't find the humor in it, we'd crumble. If our women were standing strong for us, we owed it to them to do the same. Still, my heart broke that Ryker would miss the birth of his child. And we could both miss the next two years of our kids' lives.

The judge cleared his throat, and my attention went back to his stern, no-nonsense face.

My heart thudded in my chest and then sank to my stomach. I ran my fingers over the silky tie that Grace had bought me—the tie that became part of our last lovemaking session. I hated ties, but I loved this one.

"There is no excuse for violence," he began.

I wanted to stand up and ask where he was when Hannah got the back of Cameron's hand. When Troy Mitchell beat his wife to within an inch of her life and then moved on to us kids. When a sick bastard with no conscience assaulted me.

I knew where Judge Davis was. He was probably on the golf course with Mayor Longfellow.

The judge looked around the courtroom and talked without passion. His voice was a monotone of boredom. "Given all the facts, this court finds the defendants guilty." There was a murmur behind us, but no gasps of shock or bursts of outrage because there was no way anything else could have happened. Ryker and I were stuck smack dab in the good-ole-boys network. The judge continued his sentencing in slow, stilted speech. "It's in the best interests of this community for me to sentence Ryker Savage and Silas Savage to—"

The courtroom doors swung open, and all eyes turned to Hannah and a group of women I didn't recognize. But Cameron evidently did, because his smile fell into a frown and his screw you attitude looked more like he knew he was about to get the screw.

Henry Cage, our private eye, followed behind the girls. He'd picked up the knowing smirk that Cameron had lost and pasted it onto his own face.

Cameron whispered to his lawyer, who approached the judge's bench, who called Mayor Longfellow, our lawyer, and the girls into his chambers.

Several minutes later the judge walked out and said, "I've recently been given new evidence." He looked like he'd sucked salted lemons. The gavel crashed down on his hardwood desk. "Case dismissed."

Ryker and I sat in a stupor. We had no idea what had gone down in there. All we knew was that one minute we'd been found guilty of a crime and destined to spend time in jail, and the next we were exiting the courthouse as free men.

We stood outside and kissed our girls until we were at risk of being arrested for public indecency. We had no idea how this had happened, but smiles painted our faces.

Everyone was kept in the dark until we sat in the diner for Fried Chicken Wednesday. Hannah walked over to the diner's largest booth, where we and everyone we loved and cared for were crammed together. Hannah tied her apron around her waist and said, "How's that for service?"

Ryker gave her a soft look. Probably the look Hannah had been craving for years. She pushed her hip against his side and took a seat on the few inches left at the end of the bench.

"I knew I'd never be able to win on my own, which was why I

didn't press charges." She looked over at Henry, who sat next to Marty and Mona and continued, "That man there made quick work of the mayor's son. He found a list of women in three counties who had gone out with him, and when approached, many of them spoke about some kind of abuse and a mayor who stepped in to keep it quiet. I convinced them to stand with me."

"All of those girls were his victims?" Surprise made Grace's voice travel an octave.

Hannah nodded her head. The bruise on her face had faded away, but the experience would never be far from her memory. I knew what it was like to have my choices taken away from me. That feeling of vulnerability would always live under the surface of her skin.

"We weren't so formidable as an army of one, but as a platoon, we had the power to intimidate. We told the judge that we'd all been assaulted and that in my case, you two were the pillars of the community when you came to my rescue."

"And that worked?" I asked, because I knew how the system functioned, and it was never that easy.

"Oh, no," Hannah said. "It wasn't until we threatened to go public that the mayor paid attention. He's up for re-election."

Ana leaned forward so she could see around Ryker. "But what about his future victims? You know what they say: 'A leopard never loses its spots.'"

"Cameron's spots will be in therapy for a while. It was one of the judge's requirements." She stood and looked around the table. "Fried chicken and cake for everyone?"

CHAPTER 31

GRACE

Silas had pulled out all the stops tonight. He'd bathed and fed Blue and was putting him down to sleep for the night. How lucky were we that he slept for at least six hours straight? Enough time for Silas and me to make love and sleep.

I heard Blue babble "da da da" as I walked into the bathroom for a quick shower. I could have been jealous that his first sounds weren't "ma ma ma," but all I had to do was listen to the pride in Silas's voice to realize he needed those words more than I did.

"Hurry," he called from the nursery.

"I'll be in after I shower." Silas was up to something. He'd been sneaking around all day. Then again, Silas was always up to something. He spent most of his time thinking of ways to surprise me.

Once I showered, shaved, and slathered my body in lotion, I opened the bathroom door to a path of rose petals and tea light candles lining the hallway to our bedroom. I followed the pink and red petals to the bedroom where the bedcovers were turned back, and two glasses of wine sat on the nightstand.

On the bed was a tented note. I pulled it to my chest and climbed into bed to read it.

Grace,

I don't know what to say except that I love you. Months ago, you accosted me on a sidewalk and stole a kiss along with my heart. I've made a thousand mistakes in my twenty-seven years, but you are not one of them. You're everything right in my world, and I can't imagine my life without you. And then there's Blue. He's the son I never knew I wanted, and the boy I could never turn away from. He's the hope and the light and the future. He's everything perfect in this world, and he gets that from you.

You gave me a life. You showed me love. I need you. I love you.

Love, Silas

A shadow danced in the firelight and cast its length across the floor. Silas stood in front of me wearing nothing but a smile, and I'd never seen anything look so good on a man.

"Come here, you silly man." I kissed the love note and set it on the nightstand.

"In due time." He went to his nightstand and pulled something from the drawer. Since I was on birth control, it wouldn't be a condom. It wasn't that we would be upset if I got pregnant again, but we wanted time to focus on Blue before we added another child to the mix. The only thing he could have hidden under the pillow was a bottle of lube. That idea sent a tingle down to my girly parts.

He crawled toward my body. I loved his seductions. They were always varied, but always effective. Tonight, he started at my lips and worked his way down to my hips. He trailed over the stretch marks that had once been an issue for me, but never for him.

"Do you remember when you feared showing me your body?"

I nodded as his lips traced over my hipbone and his tongue followed the fading mark to my sex, and then he moved on before I could enjoy his oral skills.

He lifted his body and cupped my breasts. "Do you remember when you told me these were less than perfect?"

I nodded as he latched on to one of my nipples and pulled it into his hot mouth, but not for long before he let it pop from between his lips. The man was killing me as he reminisced about my body.

"Do you remember the first time I told you I loved you?" He straddled my lap and brushed his lips against mine.

"Yes." I wrapped my hands around his waist so he couldn't move away from me.

"Do you remember what I promised you?" He fluttered kisses down my jawline and settled his lips on the sensitive area between my collarbone and neck.

I could hardly think, much less speak, but I found the words. "You said you'd take care of me."

"Yes, but that was after I told you that you were mine." His hard length bounced between us, and I lowered my hand to grip him. "Not yet. I have something to accomplish first."

He reached underneath his pillow for the lube and palmed it in his hand.

"You're killing me, Silas. I need you now."

He leaned back and looked deep into my eyes. "Grace, you're killing me because I don't need you now, I need you forever." He opened his palm, and sitting in the center of his big hand wasn't a bottle of lube, but a gold ring with a single diamond perched in the center of the gold band. "Most men would dress in their finest and drop to their knees, but I want you to see what you're getting." He spread his arms and smiled. "This is me, Grace. I'm not perfect. I have deep wounds inside and out. I'm not an easy man to love, but I promise to be worth it. Please say yes."

He placed the ring at the tip of my ring finger and waited.

"Are you crazy?" I knew my reaction stunned him because his eyes grew wide, but I wasn't finished. "Who else would I marry?" I pushed my finger into the ring and pulled his hand to my mouth where I whispered, "You are everything perfect in my life. You're the other half of my whole. You're the father of my son. Of course, I'll be yours —forever."

Somewhere in between "the half to my whole" and "the father of my son," Silas buried himself into my body, and he claimed me as his forever.

We lay sated in each other's arms and teetered on the precipice of sleep when the phone rang. Silas answered and flew from the bed seconds after he answered. "We're on our way."

"Ana's in labor," he said as he tossed me a change of clothes.

"We need to ask Mona to sit with Blue." I threw on my jeans and T-shirt and hopped into my knockoff Ugg boots.

I raced down to Mona's house and knocked on her door. It wasn't late—barely past ten— but no one answered.

I raced back and stopped in front of Marty's house. His lights were usually off by eight, but a glow came from the living room.

Tap

Tap

Tap

His cane tha-thunked across the floor and the door opened.

"This better be good, Grace." He looked behind him to Mona, who was running her hands through her messy pin curls.

"Oh, my God, are you guys doing it?" I couldn't wrap my head around those two going horizontal. "When did he turn into your Crixus?"

Mona stood and walked to the front door. "We're old, but we're not dead."

I shook that vision from my mind. "We need you to watch Blue. Ana's in labor." I'd never seen two ancients move so fast. It was like I'd told them there was an unlimited supply of cannoli in my house.

Silas gave them directions and wrote down phone numbers like a pro while I tossed them a couple of pillows and blankets. "You two stay out of our bed." I looked at Silas, who seemed a bit stunned by my directive. "I'll tell you later." I picked up my bag on the way out of the house.

Ana was in labor for over eight hours. Silas and I paced the hallway. I wanted to be inside the room with her, but she was afraid I'd brought the camcorder. I'd purchased a high-definition camera and had offered to tape the birth, but Ana was against me zooming in on her girly bits, high-definition or not.

Silas called Marty and Mona several times. It amazed me how alert they were, but then I remembered what I'd interrupted. If they had the energy for that, they could watch Blue.

I looked down at my ring and smiled because I knew when Silas and I were seventy or eighty, we'd be still doing it anywhere we could, even if Silas had to bend me over his walker.

We were on about our thousandth lap when I heard the cry of a baby.

Silas and I burst into the room to watch Wren being placed on his mother's chest. He was pink and chubby and beautiful with a head full of dark hair and eyes that were far too inquisitive for a baby just born.

Blue hadn't gotten a girlfriend today, he'd received a friend, and all I could think was God help us because a new generation was here, these were the new boys of Fury.

I hugged my friend and kissed her son. She picked up my hand and smiled. "You beat me to it."

I set my hand on Wren's head. "That's what sisters do. We try everything out to make sure it's good."

Silas and Ryker hugged each other and cried over the boy who would change their lives. I thought about how much my life had changed. How lucky was I to follow my friend Ana to a place called Fury to live on a street called Abundant near a sex-crazed septuagenarian who was a better mother than mine?

Relationships were different for everyone. We all fell love in our own unique way. For Ryker and Ana, it was ice and fire. They were loving each other or hating each other.

For Silas and me, it started as a lie that turned into the truth.

For Mona and Marty, it was the threat of time running out.

There was someone for everyone. They came when you least expected it.

Two days later, Ana and Ryker brought Wren home, and we sat in their living room staring at his perfection.

Ryker's phone rang. Thinking it was another congratulation call, he pressed the speaker button so we all could hear.

"Hello?"

"Ryker? It's Henry, are you sitting down?"

In fact, he was sitting down with his son cradled against his chest. "What's up, Henry?"

There was a moment of silence, and then he said, "I found your brother."

Next up is *Delivering Decker*

A SNEAK PEEK AT DELIVERING DECKER

HANNAH

His angry eyes stare back at me from strangers' faces. The memory of his laughter poisons my silent moments. His threat makes me fear for my life, but I keep reminding myself he can't hurt me anymore. He already took away everything I held dear. My courage. My hope. My ability to trust. All gone, because he didn't like the word no.

I wanted me back. Not the me that fawned over every handsome man who blew through town, but the me that stood my ground. The girl that didn't take shit from anyone. The woman who could enter hell and come out without a bead of sweat on her brow. What happened to her? What happened to me?

The bell above the diner door rang, and I jumped a foot into the air. When would the jitters end? When would I stop looking over my shoulder waiting for *him* to come after me?

Even without looking at the clock, I knew it was thirty minutes before closing, because Ana and Grace were here, dropping their dripping umbrellas by the door. They walked to the center diner booth to take their regular seats by the window. Mona shuffled behind them and slid onto the end of the cracked, red, leather bench. She was a new addition to the Hannah Banning protection squad. I silently laughed. How would an ancient blind woman help me the next time a man took his frustration out on my face?

They were looking out for me, but their concern was a bitter reminder of Cameron Longfellow's fist to my cheek, the tear to my clothes, and the disregard for my right to choose. No hadn't been a word in that man's vocabulary, but I was sure he'd been screaming it when his father sent him to a rehabilitation center in Europe.

I stopped a few booths down and topped off old man Tucker's mug. "Anything else, Bob?"

He smiled wide enough for his dentures to drop. "If I were younger Hannah, I..." I moved on before he could tell me what he would do. There were some things a girl should not have to see even in her imagination.

The pot of decaf coffee swung back and forth in one hand while three mugs hung from the fingers of the other. "Pie today?" I plopped the mugs on the table with a thud and filled them up. I reached into my apron pocket and pulled out a handful of creamers. Ana and Grace liked their coffee white and sweet. Mona took hers black like her lounge chair, or so she once told me. I had no idea what that meant.

It was the same thing each Wednesday. A cup of decaf and a piece of pie. They claimed it was girl time, but I knew it was their mothering instincts kicking in. Especially when it came to Ana. With Wren only a couple months old, her protection radar scanned everything around her, and I was a new blip.

I should've hated her for winning Ryker's heart, but I couldn't. In truth, she was perfect for him in a way I would never be. Then there was Grace. I wanted to hate her too because she had Silas. She'd swooped in and stolen one of the few remaining single men in town who was under sixty, but hating Grace was like hating chocolate. How could I hate something so sweet?

"Do you have that strawberry rhubarb pie?" Mona looked at me, but her eyes never really focused on me. They always seem to look beyond me or through me.

"Yep, I've got strawberry rhubarb and cherry and apple." With my pad in hand, I leaned against the booth and waited for them to decide.

Grace doctored her coffee with enough cream to support the dairy industry for a week. "I can't decide between apple and cherry," she said.

"Do you remember when I ordered both?" Ana looked at Grace, her shoulders shaking with laughter. "Choose one because combining them isn't a good plan."

Grace shook her head. "Chapple pie doesn't sound good. Only a pregnant woman would mix the two together." She glanced up at me. "I'll take the cherry."

"I'll take the same," Ana said. She looked around the almost empty diner. "Grab yourself a piece too and come sit with us."

Minutes later, I balanced four plates of pie on one arm and the pot of decaf and a single mug in my other hand. Grace moved next to the window and made room for me.

"Why did Tim put you on the night shift?" she asked.

I forked a piece of apple pie. "Low seniority. I take what shifts he gives me." I didn't have much choice. I needed money. Although the night shift wasn't ideal for a woman who jumped at her shadow, I couldn't turn it down. Too many people depended on me. I wouldn't let them down.

Bob rose from his seat and tossed a bill on the table. "See you soon, Hannah." That meant he'd be back when his Social Security check came in.

"Looks like Bob is sweet on you," Grace said. "I'm so glad he moved on from me. The man was always at my door with one thing or another, but he is a sweetheart."

"He's always been a good man. Those are hard to find these days." Mona wiped the red glaze from her lips and tossed her napkin to the table. "His wife was my best friend for years. We used to go see Thunder Down Under in Denver every year they came to town." Her silver-blue eyes crinkled in the corners when she smiled. "Bob would hand Avis a pile of dollar bills. He told her to enjoy herself, but to bring her appetite home. I'm not sure who loved that one day a year more, Bob or Avis. Older men usually get a six-pack of beer and a lay on their birthdays. Bob got it on his birthday *and* when the strippers came to town."

"Not a vision I want in my head, Mona." I pushed my half-eaten piece of pie away and rose from the seat. "Speaking of dollars." I walked to where Bob had sat, picked up the dollar bill he'd left, and shoved it into my pocket. "I better go and earn mine." I cleared the table and walked toward the counter.

The owl clock above the kitchen window ticked loudly. Its eyes moved from side to side, keeping time with the seconds. The double doors to the kitchen flew open, making my heart thump hard in my chest. I didn't need to wait for Cameron to come after me. I'd die of heart failure long before then.

"I'm outta here, Hannah." The cook pulled his sweat-stained bandana from his head and walked out the front door into the rain.

"What an asshole," Grace said loud enough for her voice to echo through the empty diner. "He should stay and help you lock up. We wouldn't be so worried if there was someone closing the place with you." She stabbed the last bite of her pie and shoved it into her mouth.

Once I added up their tab, I walked back and slid the bill across the table. "I don't need you here. I'm fine."

"I'm blind, sweetheart, and I can see you jump each time something startles you."

I rolled my eyes, knowing only Ana and Grace would see. "I'm fine. I don't need a damn babysitter." With their empty plates gathered in my hands, I turned and walked away.

"You need to see a therapist," Ana blurted out. "You can't get assaulted like you did and not have some lasting effects."

I looked around the diner. "The last time I looked at my benefits package, it didn't come with a mental health plan. I'm lucky to get a free meal."

"You need to talk to someone. You're wound up as tight as a trick yo-yo." Grace drained her coffee mug and slapped it back on the table. The loud noise sent my pulse racing.

"I talk to myself when I'm alone." I swiped up the cups. The owl

A SNEAK PEEK AT DELIVERING DECKER

clock hooted nine times behind me. "We're closed." I appreciated their concern, but there was nothing they could do to help me.

Mona stood and stepped in front of me. "I'm not a therapist, but I want you to come by my house tomorrow. I've found that sometimes chatting can be therapeutic. Besides, I make the best lemonade in the county."

Ana and Grace nodded in agreement.

"That's a great idea. Mona is a great sounding board. Cheapest therapy I ever received," Grace said.

Mona laughed as she walked toward the door. "I told you I was cheap, but I'm not easy." She turned and stared right through me like she saw into my wounded soul. "You better show up, or I'll have to send Marty looking for you, and he hates missing his daytime soaps."

We walked to the door. As soon as they were gone, I locked the place down like it was Fort Knox. The girls were right. I was scared to death to close the diner. On several occasions, I'd considered sleeping in Tim's cot in the back room so I didn't have to walk into a dark desolate parking lot. God only knew what was hiding behind the dumpster or the building. If I could be attacked in broad daylight, there was no telling what could happen under the shadow of night.

I married the ketchup bottles and filled the sugar containers all the while humming some senseless tune. It helped to have background noise because it filtered out the nightmare that lived in the recesses of my mind.

Get on your knees, he'd yelled that day. His fingers had tugged at my braid until I'd been forced to collapse in front of him—in front of the bulge in his pants. *You don't walk away from me.* The memory of his voice ran through my head like chainsaw. It buzzed incessantly at my self-preservation. It chipped at my self-esteem. *You're going to like it, Hannah. You might scream the first time, but then you'll beg for it.*

"*I hate you!*" I screamed. The sugar jar left my hand at a velocity I had no idea I was capable of and hit the wall with such force that it shattered into tiny shards. "Screw you, Cameron Longfellow. You are not allowed in my head anymore."

I pulled out my phone and dialed my sister because somehow her silly self made everything seem all right.

"What's up, sis?" Stacey answered with a smile attached to her voice.

"Hey, Stace, how's it going?" Already my heart rate had slowed and calmed. She had a way of putting things into perspective. She was the reason I worked this shift. She made everything worth the fear I endured. "How's school?" I missed the days when we met at the student union for coffee and bitched about our professors.

She was a year behind me. My little sister had followed me to UC Boulder for college. She'd taken up education, while I'd studied humanities. I never pictured my sister as a teacher, but then again I'd never imagined my mother to be an addict or my life's ambition to be a waitress.

"It's good. I'm gearing up for finals. I should have never taken a full load this year." Her voice held no sign of stress. Stacey didn't have to worry. That was my job as the big sister. Besides, it wasn't part of her makeup. Stacey just did what she wanted and worried about the consequences later. Long ago, we both had done that, but that was before my life turned to shit. Cameron Longfellow wasn't the beginning of my downward spiral. He was the end of my long fall into misery.

I slapped on a smile, hoping it would influence the tone of my voice. "You've got this."

Being her cheerleader was the best part of being the big sister. To focus on her meant I didn't have time to focus on me; whether it was a blessing or curse, I wasn't sure yet. But I knew the minute she walked across the stage and snagged her diploma, it would be worth it. One of us deserved a good life.

"Maybe." There was a moment of silence, which was unusual for Stacey because most days she was like a hyperactive kid who'd just devoured the entire inventory of a candy store. When she stopped to contemplate was the time I started to worry.

"What aren't you telling me?"

"Nothing. Everything is great. More than great." Her voice hit that pitch that it achieved only when she was being dishonest.

"Stace?" I kicked at the pieces of broken glass spread across the floor. "Spill it."

There was a moment of silence. "You won't believe who showed up last night." The pitch of her voice hit a nervous high C. "Mark is in town." It was so quiet I could hear the crickets beyond the closed front door chirp into the night.

"No, Stacey. You need to stay away from him. He's trouble."

"Don't worry about me. I've got this under control. He and I were always good together."

"Stace, he's bad news. Let him go," I pleaded.

It was no use. Mark was probably already shacked up in her dorm room, and she was going to get drowned in his tsunami of bullshit. The man was a menace. He had been trouble since the first day he started seeing my sister. She was seventeen when he pulled up on a motorcycle and told her to get on. That started a tumultuous relationship between the three of us. I loved Stacey, but I hated Mark Van Hauser. The day he left Stacey with a broken heart was the worst day of her life, but the best day of mine. That was nearly two years ago, and now he was back. That couldn't be good.

"I gotta go, sis. Mark is waiting downstairs."

"Stacey, don't do—" The phone went dead before I could finish my sentence. I pocketed it and went back to cleaning up my mess. Something told me I'd be cleaning up another one of Stacey's before too long. The universe wouldn't give me a damn break.

A loud bang came from the front door, and I ducked behind the counter. Peeking around the corner, I saw a man leaning on the diner door. His clothes were sopping wet. His right hand cradled his bloody left arm.

OTHER BOOKS BY KELLY COLLINS

The Boys of Fury Series

Redeeming Ryker

Saving Silas

Delivering Decker

The Boys of Fury Boxset

Wilde Love Series

Betting On Him

Betting On Her

Betting On Us

A Wilde Love Collection

GET A FREE BOOK.

Go to www.authorkellycollins.com

ABOUT THE AUTHOR

International bestselling author of more than thirty novels, Kelly Collins writes with the intention of keeping love alive. Always a romantic, she blends real-life events with her vivid imagination to create characters and stories that lovers of contemporary romance, new adult, and romantic suspense will return to again and again.

For More Information
www.authorkellycollins.com
kelly@authorkellycollins.com

ACKNOWLEDGMENTS

I always have to start with a shoutout to my family who is the reason for my everything.

Saving Silas was the logical way to proceed after Redeeming Ryker given that they are *The Boys of Fury*. The second son deserved his own story.

Although I put the words down on paper, it takes a lot of people to make them pretty. My editor gets the first round, and then it's followed by proofreaders and my ARC team. Thank you Sadye, Tiffany, Tammy, and my ARC team who give me amazing support and input.

Now, to you, the reader. Each word is chosen for you and put on the page for your enjoyment. Thank you for your continued support. Your hunger for more keeps me writing.

Kelly

Printed in Great Britain
by Amazon